I0685387

THIS IS WHAT I MUST REMEMBER
(Book 4: The Terra Nova Quartet)

by
William Gough

228 PAGES

A Gull Pond Book

ISBN: 978-1-927046432

Cover: "This Is What I Must Remember" - *acrylic paint on pine*
with balsa wood
and pine strips
Bronson Smith ©2010
http://web.mac.com/tatt2man
Book Design: Bronson Smith

Author Photo: Gary R. Snyder

With infinite thanks to an astonishing writer, Caren Moon. She's continued to believe in my books & me.

That's all a writer needs. I emerged from the forest with the 'Terra Nova Quartet,' after decades of wandering inside its pages, and she smiled in my direction.

This Is What I Must Remember

Book Four:

The concluding Novel
of
The Terra Nova Quartet

by

William Gough

"It is better to become a human than an angel.
But it is much harder work."

Spoken by Kishore Saint in the film
"The shop of the open hearted"

Kishore Saint heard the Urdu Couplet when he was a child.

There aren't any mirrors and so I have no sense of my face; no memory of ever having had one.

Even though the earth is dry, my belly and hands are wet as if dipped in blood. I'm a child again. Sometimes, I hear a cry from one of us - as if a baby is weeping; sometimes a groan - as tho' old bones are creaking against the sloped sides of a cave while I hold tight to the main bolt of an old spaceship's walls. That time of life is here & now when knees hurt, hips ache, bones grow more brittle than a sparrow dried upon the burner of a beach at low tide. Still, I feel like I'm seven years old.

There's a whisper in my left ear, as of a man telling a tale while he plays a musical saw. In my right ear, I hear a whisper. It bounces off the rippled wall and that storytelling woman has a voice of yarn. Sometimes the floor feels like the ceiling, yet, we listeners don't fall off. Then it rights itself, and I'm compelled to grip the sand beneath my left hand, while my right hand massages my belly. I know not if I am boy or girl. Here or there.

The whispers join. In the center of a circle appears a crackling fire. It shimmers, bakes, and there emerge, from the smoke, two old figures. One is a man & 'tother one's a woman. When I squint against the heat, they join (silvern in the darkness) unite fused hands & aim towards the grotto wall.

A green line of flame zaps from their pointing fingers. The cavern wall vanishes, the roof peels back

& as we spin through space, all of a tumble, our old blue moon becomes the one last sliver not eaten by hungry space. In that space, two stars fall and tumble into the gem maker of my missing eyes. All around us the rocks are singing their slow measured song.

The Girl:

Reflected Moonlight; reflected stars:
Spun by flying starfish,
charms the Ocean & crosses a reef
to hold one small girl in her arms.

Once upon this time a small girl is falling from the stars.

Drifting through space, she sleeps in black and white. As she tumbles, her thoughts are clear & her memory is perfect. Singing to the moon, she tips down & up & in & out & croons to the clouds below her.

"I am the stars," sings she, "I know who we are & everywhere we've been."

Her voice thickens; clotting as clouds while she spins like a propeller pod from spring-sprung trees. The thicker her voice gets the lower she drops. The lower she drops, the more the mountain turns. The more the mountain turns, the slower the song of the rocks becomes.

For one clear moment it is above as below. All she's ever been and all she ever will be is around her & she glows & sparks - a flesh-comet rocketing along the ocean. All the faces that she's ever been tear off & all the arms & legs & centuries of clothing & different naked bodies are ripped from her to spin by us in white and red nebula.

She tip-top-flips over the ocean, is caught by a thermal, rises, falls, skitters sideways & frisbees over the beach above the freshwater pool that bleeds into the ocean & rises again to the top of the waterfall.

"I ...

She skips along the river & changes direction;   is dragged towards the abyss.

"...am ...

The waterfall sucks her new toes; drags her beneath the water.

"...the ...

From the distance see the waterfall.

Like a jack-in-the-pulpit stamen, one foot rises upside down as the river pulls her over the edge when she enters the waterfall.

All goes from black and white to color.

" ... Stars!"

There's a splash in the pool, where the water hits the water before flowing to the water. Safely past the rocks she breathes through the sides of her neck. Her neck sparkles.

Stars are rinsed anew.

One thought – "Where am I?
Where ... are ...we?"

Words spin from her mouth; are breathed by fresh water & by the ocean. Ripples. A spinning of words.

Before the small girl who fell from the stars falls asleep she speaks to the evening star. "I wish my name; know that children get a name – that it's given them by ...parents.

I need my name."

Cuddling into a dune of cooling sand, she pulls a blanket of dried seaweed to cover her. She understands that her dreams are teachers, but isn't anxious for them to arrive. Last night, the dreams had been of dying & coming apart and blowing through snow into the sky & of stars that spoke & winds that blew throughout space & the tumble-tumbling of all around the Maypole where stars spin & go blue & green.

And though she forgets tonight all that she has come to know in whispers of the stars & although her neck, in moonlight, still has beads of galaxy-lights necklaced, and although she is naked & the wind does warm her & although she has food from trees that bend before her & all she has to do is reach her hands to thick dipped branches will dip to fill her palms with cherries: although she has all this, she longs for her name, she wants to remember what lies beneath her dreams ....knowing that she has words, and that, perhaps, she might string the words onto her necklace...

why...

...then she falls asleep.

Night flies by & back in one second & then she's again awake & it's morning & the warmest hand of the warm ocean holds her left ankle & the fingers of the tide squeeze her & when she moves her foot back she feels the fingers of the Ocean Mother & three dolphins jump before the rising sun attains its dawn & she remembers her old name & her name was Maud.

She stands up and speaks it to the Mountain.

"My name used to be... Maud.

Now, I have no name. And I have fallen from the stars. I'm aging as I go, croneing as I bow.

Yet...I am ...still...Maud."

Then all is quiet - the mountain waits.

The Boy:

Stars play on the fiddle's strings,
Each ray a new note to my ears.
My hooves are sharp; my eyes are bright
I fall and burn to give the light:
I drift into the deep night of her eyes
And while I fall, I sing.

When I was young, and of the earth, my feet slammed cross the boards of song. My saw drew moonlight from the night. I looked towards a saltshaker house; towards the shutters that bracketed bright panes.

O that window, yellow as the moon, still hangs above a clothesline stretched by forgotten sheets. Buffeted by time-winds, it shakes, but also remains. Maud was in the window. She's watching winds blow; is veiled by snow curtains. Sometimes when they wave to & fro she's young; more times she's old. Her eyes. The yellow light. She sees my eyes. She is framed by light.

That window.

I dreamed of you, in those days when we lived what was called 'a normal life.'

Falling against the painted clapboard, I smashed one day while dying in red & white bounces across the anvil of the earth & flew towards the Milky way & kept company with Pleiadian nets. Enmeshed like a glowing cod, I travelled on a time-wind, to land like a whirling tree-pod upon an icy ship. When the winds changed I sailed cross the iced vacuum of space to fall (as has been written in ancient times) as snow. Melting onto the cross-hairs of your heart, I was 4th of Julyed once more towards endless roman-candled night.

For untold years, Maud & I sang and danced in space & round & round & round we'd go until, tired of dancing, we'd fall as buttered rain once again upon the bed of midnight.

One night I dreamed in song & stamped out a jig: beat time upon the dark side of the moon & step-danced so fast (while my tiny horns held the moon) that I fell anew, arse-over-teakettles, into our new life; our joined-breath of burning ice.

Hearts aflame, we fell into the bed of the beach, and found ourselves turn old again in the hourglasses' running of such sweet drifting silica, while whispering the stories we always whisper – for we are called to sotto voce *this*; our final book.

In smoke we rise into the young folks' gathering as we, at the same time, are hurtling towards the sun, so they may hear what we distill & eat such star-dust as we've eaten & sing with the taste of star-dusting fresh upon our tongues: so hot that the fire now cools our feet.

We are back this final time, before we hydrogen-atomize it upwards into a final darkness which will be as comfy as an old jet-black sky-blanket. Black & white are all the same to me. We whisper only until these new ears, having heard their fill, may exit this always strange & yet familiar place & hand-in-hand, traverse the endless beach of endless love.

In this last desire of remembered time and space, as we fell we gathered *all* our lives like nets.

O…

…back one more time, in this sweet clime, chiming together with each other's lines. As we dropped, we rose - remembering that in this final quarter we have but one more tale to tell.

Twin antique satellites crackling through the atmosphere, we spark anew.

In earnest form (for I am Ern) I form my words on one dying writer's tongue, as in the chains of time, he rises to sing thru quartered-time, the end of our story, us and him, we & he, completing the necessary journey.

She is in a red chair.

He is in a red chair.

Their table is bare except for onion skin paper. There are grains of rice before us both. There's a microscope with a small light. Her eyes & his eyes peek at us & thru us as we burn.

Twin planets.

Our voices echo in a cave, where all, I swear is one and all; each part united.

On that last beach of sound & shingle, we fall, and watch one lonely doctor lean close to hear the earnest whisper of our conjoined story.

He also reaches for his brush, and paints a grain of rice. His large hands tremble, but will not stop until, together, we all are done right to the end.

I'm aging as I go. Aging…as I go.

The Mountain: The Star-born Motel

On this mountain at the lip of the cave is a motel that's reincarnating on the Isthmus near the edge of this groaning world.

The *Mockingbird Motel* is hidden in mist surrounded by high waves that beat against the outcrop of Barzakh. The base of this isthmus is, except for one small connecting point, encircled by an odd mixture of tides and winds.

At times, these winds and tides oppose each other. A giant mill of salt and sand, of shell & flesh-of-seaweed, and of bright red small-shelled creatures & it grinds & grinds.

The main part of the isthmus is a triangle, endlessly spiraling deep & higher than the mountain. It folds into itself again and again. If a boat approaches the dock of the motel, it finds its compass spinning. The propeller reverses direction. Smoke from anxious cigarette-smokers blows against the wind. If a plane approaches the island it is buffeted and encouraged by slipstreams & jet streams & clouds that feather to join the wings of the plane & beat, beat, beat until all the metal of the plane begins to shake & flap. Well, it's an unusual pilot who won't change direction.

If a satellite tries to take digital, infra-red, ultra-vibe, pix in hopes of a glimpse of the fabled mountain, the same clouds form a pattern of heat and cold & of light and dark - of green verdant sections & blue cool water & then those satellites puzzle over a stationary cloud and they send the information to central headquarters & (in turn) they send that information deep into the tunnels of Colorado.

Scientists climb out of their little underground carts and puzzle over electronic clipboards; hold meetings, create algorithms & nurture abstract thought (as though abstract thought were their little baby) & they suckle that growing toddler of abstract thought & have affairs, drink lattés, eat pretzels, until eventually a grown-up theory emerges & they test it and it doesn't work & they are demoted & they lose their Shanahan Ridge houses & their expensive cars are repossessed. They regret having followed Science & they long for Frat parties when the world seemed as if it could be conquered by mere alchemy. Before they consider this hour to be a dreadful hour, that thought drifts away & they move back in with their old & embittered parents in Gunbarrel.

But the distant mountain remains & they have no idea that it *is* still possible to check into the totally unexpected motel; to leave behind boats & outboards, planes & wings, cars & engines, directions & maps, plans & exit routes, banks & accounts, credit & cards. Such minds need credit cards, accounts, banks, exits, best routes, plans & maps & directions & wings altogether & planes & engines and boats.

Simple? Yes!

This isthmus (with its one mountain) has no grid of power-lines; it has no gauges. The only steam comes from a hot-spring network that pulses beneath the island while hissing serpentine songs to swaying Sea Lions. This mountain likes being alone by the sea. Winds blow from different time directions.

Those winds are time-winds, not just West-Nor-West, but *1958* West-Nor-West. It's that precise here. Parts of the shoreline have collapsed houses from 1957, others (inland) are from 1854, some from the late 90s, or 2011; still more drop in from some undetermined future time. Cables are dead & antennae are buckled. At morning & in deep night the time-winds blow. And of course they howl over the ear canal of hidden caves.

If you stand there, you can hold your hand to the sky & watch your palm fade & deepen & fingers grow longer & then shorter. Sometimes it will become the hand of a little girl, or of a teenage boy; sometimes red or yellow & other times white, all shifting through black & powdered cream to a full moon when your hand turns deep blue and you dress in yellow and the yellow silk whips around your changing blue body and you feel it press and hold and enter and exit.

O...

...it swirls & threads through your veins & you web your hand towards the moon and it flows over cobalt serpentine veins. Sometime when you write, you're a little girl, or a little boy. Other times, an old man, an old woman. In the morning when you sit at your table you're a man, at night you're a woman. Occasionally you're an abandoned village & you invite time-winds to sing shades of peeling & fresh paint thru your broken picket fences. Sometimes you speak with the voice of granite, other times you sing with the voice of a spruce tree. The time-winds do shape you.

You know.

Those winds.

Near the abandoned town, past the gap-toothed picket fences & across from a wild forest within smiling distance of the cave of the Sea Lions, is formed a small motel.

Years of smog and wind and heat and blasting rain have left behind the shadow of the letters; only the shadow. The old neon sign that was a part of what this motel was once when it sang to the Los Angeles sky, is on far and away planets & stars re-born & leaves behind only the clips that (once in the future) held the old sign. In the past it will hold the neon tubing. Even if there were no faded letters a child could play connect-the-dashes. M-o-c-k-i-n-g-b-i-r-d space M-o-t-e-l.

There's a new sign woven of broom that was cut while green; threaded until it went brown and gray with black pods that locked like steel around an arboreal ancient-wizard's tree-beard, filled with nests of the first tourists to check into the motel – the englobulated birds. In the courtyard is a salt-box house. It's obscured by mist.

White clapboard, with a red-paint smear down the side.

City sparrows blown out of concrete streets tumbled wing-over-tails when snow covered much of the world except for the place of memory where spring & summer mixed into fall & winter, and were blown, snow left behind on other-time earth at the end of that world, past end-time & start-time towards the no-time Mockingbird Motel.

See the latest arrivals, a flock of Grackles complaining as usual while they fling themselves past a cloud of Brewer's Blackbirds. They arrive in a bursting cloud, find nests at the motel & set up shop & chirp & burp & fart & fling worms back and forth. Some land on the roof of the salt-box wooden delight that's set in the expanding courtyard: Maud's house. Name lifted again and again, yet the little house still shakes & trembles, while nesting sparrows stay put. Board by board one small house builds itself in the shadow of the motel.

The Mockingbird Motel, itself, always awaits.

A witch's-wedding-broom, made of broom, hangs above the door & has mugwort woven through it. Primrose is falling. Honeysuckle grows up the walls & there are footprints on the way to the front door & the footprints are of a small girl & they go to the door, they go around the motel. They vanish by a window left open.

They're followed by small hoof prints, treading an odd pattern.

Then they emerge out the other side, heading towards the cave – aging as they go, old feet, old hooves, cutting wide & cutting deep in the moss that time-lapses, displaying macro-detail after macro-detail in incremental ageing's speed-up. Almost like another Universe's Foxtrot. Listen to them – you can hear the music of a buckled saw; of a mandolin.

At the waterfall of memory, the spray is high and droplets are blown by a new wind into the face of the sun & decorate the cheeks of the moon & deepen inside the motel & sprinkle into a sweet & delicate layer of dust; landing as small reverse-freckles. The new register now looks old & faded time-winds enter the window of the motel & blow along the halls & the fresh vivid carpet fades & spider webs are spun & spiders lower themselves, rappelling down like a bad action film & they web together the register's pen & the sign-in register itself. Of all the doors in the motel (besides the front door) only one door is closed, and from behind it, at exactly the same time as old steps go towards the cave, even older steps emerge from the cave & a small girl's voice is singing.

O...

...here, all time is at once.

Time-winds pause - to listen.

As breezes cease, light-hooks begin to laser-claw a vast shadow. Sea Lions attend, rats stop making nests: even grackles grow silent.

There's the sound of creaking wood against creaking wood & of rhythmic oar-lock motions & of voices dream-talking about Huck Finn & there's the sound of a piano.

The ocean listens; clouds form a corridor & trees lean against each other to shape forgotten trails. Birds tilt their heads as the giant worm of the sky arrives just in time for lunch.

Moss shivers. Steps fade.

Clapboard claps wooden hands together. Wells fill. Light spills again. Time shifts.

And the wind blows dust from the register.

It is time.

Here we come, the all of us.

O

it's time

&

we're glad you called.
It is time.

Time spins us in a bony hand, and I cannot see my face. But, now I know this to be the book we're all writing in a cave. This is the one we'll miniaturize on grains of rice.

These pages are about all of us: Arrow & Moloch & Music Girl & Stephen & Yemaya. It's about Gabriel and Thomas Zarov, about the good doctor, about Eve (born as Lilith), about the music girl becoming Luna di Luna, and...all of us... are becoming us. We'll learn each other's true names as the fire burns down. Sometimes the Man in the Black & Blue Jacket (the man with stars as blazer buttons) visits. And there's always Queen Mab & her attendants.

One of all of them is me. I don't know yet which me I am. If I write, I'll learn which one, for letters are in my veins and, when I hold my fingers towards the light & let the words blow like wind across the shells of my ears, I can almost see my face, can rub my parchment skin, taste my onion skin. So far I have not learned which one I am, but I feel growing pains, my legs shift straighter every day, the air is thinning enough to breathe and, sometimes, as if ten mirrors hang before, behind, over & under & behind my widening eyes, I almost catch a glimpse of me. When I look down towards my hand, it curls, as if to hold a quill. So far I can see only their memory-mirrored faces

– the more the old man & woman in the one body talk, the more my ears ring and sing.

The more the storyteller yarns, the more we form. The more we form, the more we write & one day, as we dream, we'll move & walk & leave the cave & talk with each other like we used to talk. We'll dance on the beach and walk to the mainland and then, while holding hands, we'll tell you more.

Right now, one of us paints, and the brush is to the grain, and another's hissing spray-paint-can will paint the wall of the cave and it does smear & the paint has crystals mixed with the pigment. O, you may swear that I can hear it sing.

We need a quill – we need red ink.

The First Grain Of Rice

Suppose you've been eating a bowl of plain rice in a cheap restaurant.

On the end of the left chopstick is a sudden grain of rice with scarlet writing. You discover that the rice was gathered from a floating bottle & you find it so odd that you take it home & borrow (perhaps from a curious nephew) a microscope and then you adjust a delicate light and set the grain of rice upon a glass-slide beneath the lens and see, startled by the very sight of your encircled eye, words.

You begin to write down what you're reading from this grain of rice.

The transcribing of what's written on this first grain of rice takes you years & you send out for food & people wonder where you've gone. Your money runs out. Yet you stay in this room where you have one table and a red chair & you turn from beginning to end, ever so slowly, this grain of rice.

One day, forgotten by everyone, except stubborn bill collectors, you emerge from your room. In your hand, written in bold ink, are your own words looped on sheets of onion skin paper. Over the years your hand has become steady; your writing as clean and true as a girl's whistle heard over a lake – true enough to shiver the fog.

And you hold the pages up.

The sun sends one ray of light through the banks of fog. That ray smokes across the paper. Words fill in the open space in the clouds; words gather – a swarm of letter-bees of yellow light and velvet darkness. The netting cluster buzzes, bees in flight through the fog. The mist closes; your hand is empty. Your microscope forgotten, you take the grain of rice which you wished to share with the world and you eat it.

As you bite down, your eyes become twin suns over a pale moon and your blood gives a powerful surge. Your forehead vanishes, an eye emerges and dominates the brow-scape looking at me.

I look into your eye and scribble my own note.

I am writing this book for you.

Arrow

Bones rattle in Cascade Locks.
Arrow learns how he may fly,
in words, from Oregon,
to escape life's hard knocks.

"Cascade Locks sucks!"
        Words leave the spray can – crazy-string hanging letters on anything where letters may hang. Pleased with his spray-painted handwriting because it looks so sloppy & equally happy that the cops don't spot him, Arrow leans back, dropping his first spray can – sending paint over the pavement, in a zigzag cut.

He makes, on this night, a decision to go missing; to fly through light, high enough to arc over the park, shoot like a star through the dark – explode into Roman-Candle light like a paint-can-pixel-burst (to be the first, he thinks, to fly past the *cul d'sac* speed of light and go through the moon to what's hidden on the other side, grabbing the trapeze bar that swings from stars, surfing the cosmic tide, blasting a cave into his heart and climbing inside.)

He doesn't give a shit about fine particles of spray-paint drifting towards him. He's in deep focus – leaning at the perfect angle, drawing out words on the wall; creating a wavering image of a one-eyed skateboarding Martian – he's busy paint-spraying green-lit parsley sprig-bursts on the wall.

Doesn't care if he's seen, caught, goes to jail with all the townsfolk saying, "We knew it would come to this. His mother, his father, they really ought to have, ...well, if they'd only been, more caring!" Sucking in breath, rolling their eyes like a bizarre Cascade Locks version of a Greek Chorus (not worried about anyone mocking them for doing the choral stride) the townsfolk continuing to chant, while marching their endless street, "This comes as no surprise. This, in our measured opinion, comes as no surprise."

Hearing in his mind, their words, Arrow spray-paints more. This unfeathered boy doesn't care about anything and he's right not to care. His father is out drinking draft beer & eating cheap steak rare. The pooled blood of the steak has chilled in red and white bubbles; his French fries stick to the plate. A neon sign beating against the night washes pink across his brain.

This dad can't eat it all & so he drinks some more. Later he'll stagger out the door so angry and so sad that he'll, in his fuming sorrow, seek his sorry son, Arrow & loosen the belt-whip to hit, slash & snap. His eyes will become a beating red light: beating in a scarlet stare strong and cutting. Sharp as a steak knife & straight as an arrow at Arrow. It's the "Here's the belt, boy!" kind of dad – the unkind kind of dad.

Arrow's mother (whose best action in her life was to name this kid) has long been gone; a free spirit, no one's wife, mother to no one. Tubes tied. Mother to nar other. Leaving her family of birth she left no other sisters or brothers for Arrow.

No siblings shake in the wind which rocks an old RV, where she feels it's grand to be heading for a gathering somewhere south of Tombstone. Easter Island figure strapped above the front bumper. No radio, no TV, no phone: just her and the coyotes, on their own, singing and yipping songs that the moon coaxes from her gut. O yes, that mother – that long vanished woman – her! She's her own rainbow. That's his mom.

Arrow received his yearly postcard from her this morning. It didn't have a stamp on it but got to him anyway. It said simply "I still luv you Arrow! Sorry I couldn't hang to see what you've become; your dad was too much of a fighter for me to stay another month, or week or night. Fly true, fly straight. You are a writer. Go and write."

Arrow remembers this postcard & writes a spray-painted poem in orange letters:

> - *Fuk You Cascade Locks.*
> *I write -*
> *- Fuk you on this and every night. -*
> *I am a writer*
> *riter*
> *F – u – k*
> *u*

He peers towards the moon that hangs over empty parks. Wipes his hand across his face. Orange paint makes his jaw glow in the dark. Poem done, he drops this spray can (which is covered in orange and green fingerprints.)

"Isn't anything ever going to happen?"

Looking back at the full moon he speaks to it.

"You there looking at me all the time. Is this it? 'Cause if it is I'm pissed. No crime I can commit could ever erase this pissed-off feeling. Make something happen. Now!"

The moon trails her spray-painting fingers across his face; scraping nail-pixels vivid on his cheeks but he doesn't see this. There is, however, a sudden reek of cheese – because the moon does love a joke. When speaking to your heart she'll make you smile, reveling in what lies beneath the day. She'll sing in that broadband voice of hers, run her fingers across your face, and lick the back of your neck until you say, "It's getting cold...I must go in."

But, oh, if you remained. Just took another toke. If, like the trout, you found a stream beneath the current where the temperature is a steady four degrees Celsius & stayed & fish-face-first, you felt the water pour deep moonlight past your ears – why then you'd be like Arrow & spray-paint your way from Cascade Locks ...

... O ...

... you'd never stop until you ended up inside this book or wrote your own volume of your own quartet and then, twirled around by voices from the sky, you'd look the full moon in the face until she dropped her shawl. She'd hop like a rabbit to play inside the cage of your chest and you would fly between her ribs & be born with Arrow.

Join the woman in the shawl; the one who lives inside the moon. Leap into the zero point and out the other side and so will I.

But right now, it's enough to know the moon spray-paints Arrow's face, letting the world know poets write with spray-paint-tins-&-paint-tin-pens. Poets do skate endlessly on a skateboard of words. Poets must always be absurd, falling through sidewalks, melting into the cracks, going word-deep into the earth. What is seen there tickles remembrance, until the sound of memory's mirth gives birth to Arrow and all his crew...

... O ...

...come skate with us, spray-paint naked against the moon.

Close your eyes, wave your arms like they're seaweed, for we will follow Arrow to the center of the earth & we would follow Arrow to the center of the moon.

His skateboard rattles past an alleyway, and something there catches his eye, enough to, heel down, spin around; turn around. Skating back to take a look, he sees it's only an alley. He stares in, not one to fear, but feels on his back chill air running goose bumps all along his spine. Thoracic & brain freeze. Brrr...could have sworn he saw, in the alleyway, a fire set in a cave & around it (slumped) seven children looking into the fire. Ten mirrors all around, a geodesic dome spinning in space.

He closes his eyes, remembers clearly what he saw. Blink – eyes open.

No cave. No space-traversing dome. Shrugs. Thinks it might be the aftereffects of the last rave.

And skates on.

From the alleyway – blink – a pulse of fire light, the murmur of whispers.

Blink.

This morning in the cave, when we opened our eyes, there were a series of paintings on the wall. One replacing another. A skateboarding boy. A woman in bed, sleep mask in place. A doctor sleeping next to a sleeping patient. A girl with flaming hair playing a green piano. A man (all in white) next to her, joining in. A Newfoundland pony in 1957 snow trudging in an off-kilter beat as it listens to music. A jumbo jet against the sun. A sink of dishes overflowing.

A country singer, hair as wild as an old Curly Kate, slams hand over guitar, and dancing around her is a short-order cook in stained apron; a woman in a muu-muu and they dance. They sing. We hear the melting painting sing:

Down on the Labrador, me by's, Down on the Labrador.
Down on the Labrador, me by's, Down on the Labrador.
Down on the Labrador, me by's, Down on the Labrador.
Down on the Labrador, me by's, Down on the Labrador.

The song keeps looping. Overtones on top of each other like an Origami construct of Gerald S. Doyle's infinite songbooks. Green. Black. Green. Black.

As we watch, one layer dissolves & then another & another & beneath each layer there's a newer layer, so we can see what will happen to the book that's to be transcribed from the grains of rice rescued from the bottle.

All this will happen in a single room, bare, except for a jar of rice on a pine table with one red chair next to it. The chair is turned to look out a dirty window. I see this room, and suspect it may become mine.

In future & past time there's a film crew entering the room & looking for a location in an movie about being lonely; about living in urban caves. The director looks around and laughs. "Here's a good way to end up. Look lively, lads or this could become your final room." The Locations Manager laughs.

One crewmember hangs back, looks out the window, sees what I see; the sidewalk filled with light: illuminated faces of people as they float through their lives. Heads resembling electric eggs.

He doesn't look at walls. Nope, he watches paint that's filled with crystal and pigment, and without a word, swears (in pictures to himself) that one day he'll make a film of this room, will assemble it from bits and pieces, his heart pumping light. He reads odd letters and signs jotted down. *CB 31 45 02 907/ AC 20 54 18 566/ AB 37 22 38 527.*

"What the hell?" he wonders. There's an itch between his eyebrows.

He says nothing because he works for the Bureaucracy of the Arts (in early days when government was first starting to take over creativity: when scripts engendered meetings, and those meetings created even more meetings, and civil-service executives of The Arts flew to Cannes and drank coffee and talked big talk. Those days.) Once that was his dream. But, now his heart beats, beats, beats and joins the pulsing light of all who are on the streets. More in common with anyone in a food bank than anyone chugging chilled mineral water.

The director is puzzled why this crewmember doesn't laugh at his joke. Instead, the man, knowing that speech is required by lazy ears, observes that someone "greater than all of us" is living in this barren room.

"Greater than us?" The director laughs again. A pleasant laugh. He likes a joke, and now he thinks that he's heard one. Greater than us? In such an empty room? Not a book to be seen. Good one.

We watch the film crew melt and fade; years burn & time-smoke fills our cave.

When it clears, we see one painting & it's of the book we're all writing. Just past the red ochre of the smeared bison, next to the deer with the Moukalite crystal eyes & under the sweet talons of the bird people, there is this book –

and already I know more about that story than I know about myself.

Mab:

The professor asks the Moon, "What's beneath the floorboards.

O…

…what makes a distant skateboard go clik-clatter-clik in the sky?

O…

…what spins wheels against the stars like thunder?
…Where am I?"
…asks the professor.

Although she doesn't know the answer, she knows enough to ask the question of where her life may be sliding and where it came from gliding over words of "Where? Where! Where did it (whatever it was) go?"

She stands a moment by the counter, wondering who fills her sink with dishes? And who left the tap drip-drip-drop-dripping so much softer than the shadow of a dog running between the moon and the soft ferns of a Northwest rain forest plink-plinking in the filling sink?

Past sounds of hissing, wheels spinning, voices blending with the creak of the world – the world that tonight will shoot Arrow towards the moon.

"Soon," the professor thinks, "my sink will overflow. "

Will she ever, herself, overflow?

"When it does, I will remember. Perhaps the moon may do my dishes. Perhaps I will learn about the 'where' and 'when' and 'what' and 'why' and..."

She stops; forgets her words and forgets her sink; thinking this moment is somehow absurd.

The dishes.

The thin grease eating up the suds. The skin of grease becoming skin covering an itch.

"Something there is beneath the floorboards – that I must deal with. Something as soft as the shadow of a long-gone dog."

Descending the cellar stairs. Past the leaking sink. Down to where secrets live, she ignores water plashing over sideboards unto the floor. The stairs give and creak like sponge toffee crunched & ground between the teeth. By midnight, at the tuning & turning of the full moon, more water spreads across the floor & cascades down the cellar stairs in tiny flowing Gumby-animated oceans. Once more, she does no more than observe, serene as she hears a distant skateboard rattle near the moon.

"Arrow" she thinks. "Who is Arrow?"

Parting curtains of sound.

Sound does sky-wheel a Catherine-wheel-spin over her forehead along her brows down into her blue eyes spilling out over the eyes into the ears, spin-wheeling sounds. Outside her home, moon dusts clouds. Dust drifts dandruff across her dark shoulders when she opens the cellar window set in the old coal-scuttle hatch. She's cold tonight & the cellar window opens like the mouth of a chilled hippo saying "Ah" to a dentist in the sky. Light leaves the window the same way it drifts from a cave.

Looking towards the moon, her years of restraint now gone, she lifts her head & wonders what in the name of Merciful Merniva is happening. Unexpected snow dots her shoulders while water blunders up her ankles. She dreams of a plane of glass that will fly her to the stars & comic-book-slams her wrists together to make that happen.

"What trick is this," puzzles she, "where a skateboard sound may rattle the moon? What trick is this where I'm alone & don't give a shit if neighbors fail to muzzle their fierce howling dogs? Nor do I care who I am, where I come from, who I used to be, who I may become, nor what parts add up to the final sum of who I am. I'm through with bullshit."

She pauses "I repeat myself ... The 'I'..." She pauses again. "...The 'I' who will be...melting in the moon..."

Hearing what she's just said, the professor quivers. The water grows higher, small waves grab her by the ankles. She gasps for breath before releasing her cry.

Her cry is of a wolf. She is a lone wolf standing in the circle of the moon; the circle that cages the blue rabbit.

"Why, I am Mab. My name is Mab! I am Wolf-song Mab. Queen of the Faeries...Mab."

She howls at the circle of the moon, so powerful is the remembering of her name. Her name wavers towards the center of the moon. When she howls again, cords in her neck slant/tighten like skateboard ramps.

The sound cave-echoes.

Water rises and falls in far-off Cascade Locks to the rattle of skateboard bones. The rattle ricochets off her door, a pin-ball bullet. She climbs out the open window.

Feet cold, wet, now chilling, she stands on powdered autumn snow. Alone, head uplifted. Holding in her glasses the reflected image of the moon she howls until the neighbors call for help. She has no fear of neighbors nor of police.

"Destiny..." she thinks & amends the thought, "...Fate...is very, very near."

She shivers, her howl dying as a growl.

Her growling ends.

All I really know in this cave, is that I can write, although I can't remember learning to read (at least this time back on earth).

What I recall, from my life before the life before the cave, is that one day I was sitting with a newspaper, reading aloud *The Lone Ranger*. "He memorized it" said my father. "Read something else!" And I froze. When they'd gone away laughing, I went back to reading.

Denny Dimwit was my favorite character as I'd been called that when I was earth-born, my head squeezed to its coned Capet-point (wall-to-wall-Capet – O – that was my joke of the life before.) It comes back to me: the memories. But I don't yet have a name. Haven't got the point this time round. It blew away from me the way my working life drifted, when I died on & in film.

The storyteller talks & as she does I learn the future history of our books. It doesn't bother me: Nothing bothers me. I cannot see my body, I don't know if I have a head, and yet I keep on writing – it's the one thing I know and my hands won't stop. I look behind and see a bit of the future.

After decades of repair, or neglect of life in second-and-third-and-more-hand bookstores, there's to be the goodwill journey for this & other books; after the fluorescent vibe of second-hand stores, the path to the dump, the burning & crackle & dull stop-the-fire, cigarette-butt-out, in-a-saucer-of-cold-tea reading.

After that journey, there's the burring of small insects; book-lice coming home, the prodigal book louse – home at last to daddy and mommy who are waiting with their moist antennae a-peeking over the edge of a battered duct-taped book. O sweet prophets of the printed page.

Hang on book-lice, we're just getting going. First we read, then you eat.

That tree in the forest – (that tree for sure) – see it fall slowly as a startled eyelash does fall from a great height into a sacred net of eyelashes. When it falls it will take you with it even if you are not there. That tree is now falling on this town.

London Bridge is on a raft at long last.

Falling, falling, falling down.

That tree.

And all awaits the inevitable visit.

We are falling, spinning, feather-people & we land soft on the mountain on both splayed feet, our hands against paper, our brow smudged with ink.

We are pages in a book.

When we're pages in an e-book, we're pixel-blown away when the satellites go boom. Boom. Like a spring-sprung expanding mechanical heart made by 12th century clock-makers. When that clockwork heart stops, all Facebooked friends & friends of friends of friends will be erased as satellites expand. Gone to pixel dust. Faster than a tweet. Quicker than you may smile.

"What was that?" the book-lice will wonder. Look up, and then down. Go back to chomping on the final letter. Z is for zero.

And we sing, and we groan. We feel our throats do the grape-jelly tremble. All of us move slow & slower & then we stop, our hands covered with sand. Those sandy hands reach out and, ever so slowly, we turn the pages and, rapid as the blink of a newt, we enter and slow the words, and *see*, on the first horizon, what we are meant to see.

Eat the first grain of rice.

That's what Mab hears. That's what she does. That's what she reads.

Mab sticks out her tongue. Surprised at first by the dropping of the grain upon the tongue, she reaches in & takes it off. Goes to get her own magnifying glass.

Forgets.

Goes to her books. Swears she can hear the wood lice reading.

The moon glows, snow-topped mountains are covered in rice storms. She picks up the magnifying glass.

Rice blows against the window.

The moon watches. As usual.

Gabriel:

*Gabriel is adrift
in what will prove for him to be
the elusive field of lost memory.*

Gabriel is alone in the middle of a meadow & his traveling companions have melted away. No memories remain of the way their faces looked before they vanished. No memory of what they called him. It's enough that he's forgotten his past, the details of his life, the fame.

Today's the day he feels one more memory slip away from him and, as it goes, take with it his name. The only sign that humans have ever been in this grassland is the wake of his own trail.

All his life Gabriel has been puzzled, yet pretended he wasn't puzzled. Not wanting to look in any way absurd, he always has a keen sense that he might be observed. Wishing to do nothing that might bring shame, that might make him look ridiculous, he composes himself so it will look as if this is where he'd planned to be; as if this were the most natural thing in the world – no need to fuss. Being in the middle of a strange meadow, all his friends melted (leaving nary a puddle of water) yeah – he doesn't want to make it look like there might be something…strange.

"It could happen," his expression says, "to the very, very best of us."

Alone in the middle of a field at the edge of the forest on the top of one mountain across from another he wonders how there could be another mountain. There wasn't one there before. And it's an exact duplicate. Could it all be done with mirrors? Big mirrors?

Gabriel remains dazed. Is this the land where he's finally lost his mind? A squirrel leaps through his vision to vanish behind an outcrop of sheered rock that's bent and buckled in the center of the mountain. The squirrel reemerges, bounding past a shale knoll that, until now, Gabriel hasn't noticed. It feels as if the squirrel rips through him though it's many feet away. His body has some kind of sensor – a field in a field. He looks at the mirror and sees himself looking back. He wonders how there could be a mirror this big. He waves to himself.

He waves back from the other mountain plateau.

He almost smiles but, as someone might be watching, Gabriel stops waving. He sneaks another quick glance at the mirrored mountain. The other guy glances back. This time neither one waves.

There could be… who knows what there could be? He settles on a knoll that now undulates across the center of the field. Here the earth swells, like the ceiling of a cave. There's a murmuring, whispering sound from the earth beneath.

Gabriel wears a long flowing robe fastened with an elaborate sash & if he were the kind of man who didn't mind being naked in the wilderness he'd yield & strip everything off. He can't quite remember how this has come to pass – how he's ended up sitting on an outcrop of rock in the middle of a strange field. This doesn't feel like an illusion; the knoll is cold and rocky on his ass.

He's used to forgetting things always. Even as a child on one mild winter's day at the age of seven he'd stood in the center of the kitchen, in the first house that existed in his memory where his mother asked again, and again, and again, "What – are – you – supposed – to – tell – me?"

At that time his silence grew profound. He understood he could never answer such odd questions, so he remained quiet and, during these moments, his mother evolved a belief (and assorted sub-species of this belief) that he was a stubborn & sour-tempered boy.

But truth was, he'd forgotten where he'd been; had forgotten all errands & what he was supposed to learn from all that he'd seen. He'd already, at this age, when other boys ran free, forgotten how to feel joy. Forgotten at seven quite how to be a seven-year old boy.

Dust blows across the courtyard of the Mockingbird Motel.

Re-formation. All is still, as still as dust on paintings of apples in a still life hanging over the mantle of a Duke's forgotten mansion, as dusty as the back yard of a misplaced Shaughnessy big house. Re-birth. There's one beam of light emerging from the cave on the nearby hill.

The wind tears away brush & then rolls tumbleweed down the slope from the smoke vent and, after one black cloud of smoke emerges to be ripped into tatters & then is spliced by tidy breezes, there's a wavering orange shaft of light hanging down from the mountain: an undulating serpent of light.

Like a polypropylene rope it attaches to the fountain in the center of the motel courtyard's circular well. It quivers. Flying embers & smoke & cinders & flankers & sparks begin to drift towards grey & dry clapboard.

They smash against the walls & burst into brilliancy. Nothing catches fire, but the boards are licked by light. Once. Twice. The Mockingbird Motel sign grows neon tubing, then blinks on.

More sparks & they drift to Maud's house, to hang around like faeries inside a marigold bush. Light blink around the house. A window clicks the switch for its own light. Yellow in the grey. Blinking at the smoky night.

Letters reform. Words blink back.

Eventually Gabriel was punished for forgetting; was beaten and sent to bed. Although he did go ahead and cry until his eyes were empty, red, hot & dry, he could not remember what he was supposed to tell or not tell his mother. In his distant childhood (so late in the night) Gabriel (without a sigh) forgot the beatings.

The forgetting of his dreams was always easy, rolling dust-bunnies – hidden under his rumpled bed. In the morning, he'd leave his quilt-cave, throwing off the roof of covers & rush down the stairs to the smell of crunchy bacon.

He'd throw his arms around his mother as if she were the kind of mother who would care.

And although she never was the sort of mother who'd hug back, she stopped for a while, on this particular morning, being mean, and gave him extra bacon to show she cared.

He'd chewed the bacon, munched on blackened toast. It was burned because she held the wire rack on the hottest part of the old stove & he liked the taste of carbonated toast.

His mother smoked & smiled & drank nail-bending coffee, delighting (as much as she could delight) in how much he ate. As soon as his plate emptied, she'd heap it full again, go to the stove, lift the damper, put a long sliver of wood into the flames & the sliver would sputter & then flare & she'd light her fresh cigarette. The flame would be next to her nose, and that got his attention. Dropping the wood back into the flames, she replaced the lid with a clank, sucked down the smoke & poured molasses in strong coffee & gave it to her son.

"This will be sweet I suppose, " she'd said.

The smoke, when she blew it out through her nostrils, tacked across reheated hotcakes. But Gabriel was a boy who'd slept with clear dreams and already forgotten about yesterday, so he was happy & didn't mind the taste of smoke moleculed into desiccated hotcakes. He liked the smell of cigarettes mixing with his mother's perfume; the way smoke rolled & spilled & disintegrated like total recall shaken in a bar.

When his father came downstairs, Gabriel stopped eating with his mouth open (even though food tastes so much better that way!) and he ceased swinging his feet back & forth. His father hated, on even the best day, seeing feet swing and would be likely to give him a clout on the side of the head for irritating him deliberately. No warning, no apology – just a clout.

Released from childhood's realm, but captured deep in current time, finding himself in a strange place with no knowledge of how he got there, or even where he has come from, Gabriel gazes at the sky that rests on the snow-melted mountain meadow where he sits.

A grown man, no longer a boy, he takes the time to look around, to lift his gaze from the ground to the sky. One cloud turns into a puff of cigarette smoke. Inside the smoke is the image of the other mountain. So high that – well, birds need backpacks and oxygen masks, or so Gabriel believes. The cloud dissolves, disappearing into a remembered cry & there's only blue sky.

Looking down again, Gabriel wonders where he might be. A wind wavers the tall grass, blowing through him, tearing his edges, whistling through parted space left by the jumping squirrel. No one is near.

He smokes & the uncurling blue & grey now flows into clouds smudging the once clear blue of the sky. Only one thing is written in his notebook.

"This is what I must remember or I will die."

The earth murmurs again. The very same words settle like sediment inside a test tube. The way smoke soaks into dry hotcakes, spelling out destiny. The *Denny's* fortune cookie.

Moloch:

Hidden in the most obvious place;/ a purloined letter of blood
and flesh/ placed on a shelf of time and space/
Moloch quickly writes;
a look of hunger fixed upon his face.

Day Log

"...He is shivering and...I don't understand what makes him
shiver... It's so hot in here that his ass should melt before dawn
and that's how long I'm here – long enough to melt while I watch
this fucker.

I begin to wonder if I should kill him now and save him the life
that makes him quiver? Perhaps I should wait? I know he can't see
me. I am like the bee yes – yes I am. When I sting I die. Let it pass,
because of the glory of the stinging.

Time for him to remember."
He shouts.
"Now!"

His eyes close; head drops down to his sleeping chest until his clipboard hits the floor. Jumping to his feet, startled, Doctor Summers becomes just another being, looking around to make sure he's not observed.

Relieved to see that he's not, the good doctor picks up the clipboard and reads, amazed, what is set down.

"What the hell does "glory of the stinging" mean? Who wrote that!? Some version of me?" A frown.

Another casual glance around & he departs while shredding the paper, wondering – wondering: Where is Gabriel?

Where?

Arrow has no proof of it but when things do happen; when he finds his short life almost at its end – when the night races towards him later, when he misses his mother, & enters the tunnel to the place inside his deepest mind, he will recall *this* moment and know the moon heard him and answered.

The folding bellows of the universe has Arrow in its neck.

Slamming his green dotted skateboard to the pavement Arrow begins the long sweep through the town. It is not early, it certainly is not late but he's the only person who rolls bones down the angled streets of Cascade Locks, through town, towards the river where the gate keepers & their gates keep the town away from all that gates keep out... Water.

Water, penned in its move towards the gorge, is transformed through schemes of engineers to be a fivefold-form-calm-stream moving in rational fashion over a series of logically-locked-&-unlocked, computer-driven-binary-up-and-binary-down-clicked-and-un-clicked logical gates.

Rational is not for Arrow. He likes it when water rushes, tears, overflows, spins, makes mud pies along the banks. He prefers zeros to ones.

Arrow's skin is bronze; hair flying behind him in bleached thin dreadlocks. Time-winds blow against his dry face. The moon reflects from slanted eyes.

"Goddamn, you look more like a lizard than a boy" his father always says to him.

"Goddamn, I feel more like a lizard than a boy," is what he said back to his father last night. Instead of hitting him, his dad laughed; laughed so hard he had to puke. However, because he was in stiches, he did not nuke his kid.

Arrow feels the rumble of the skateboard through his feet. His knees are as loose and easy as his balance. He widens his arms like a landing seagull, holds spray cans in his claws, aiming the spray downward as the board flies along the street. There's two wobbly fluorescent yellow line unpeeling behind him as the cans hiss-spurts & sigh-empties.

– I am the lizard – is what he thinks & he hunkers down bending at the knees until he looks in the moonlight like a lizard on a skateboard in a too small town.

Clank, clank. Round the corner.

His shadow follows him: its reptilian tail a knobbled thin sail tacking across the shadows feeling reborn – new. He looks at the moon and shouts "I am the lizard, and the lizard says 'fuck you'."

The sound of rushing water, the hum of neon signs on beer halls. A distant car cranks its starting motor until it finally stops. Two lovers who have nowhere else to go stop looking at the water & then stare at themselves & then sigh, eye-to-eye, reflected in each other's eyes. Pupils widen, dark night, moon light. Each one kisses the other. Kisses deep and slow, feeling past low gear position as buttons unbutton. The girl sucks her lover's lips easing his hand from her hips. Leans back to take a look.

"I love you."

"Yeah" he replies "I guess you do," just another guy who doesn't know what else to say.

The car has a vanilla-scented cardboard tree hanging off the mirror. It trembles as the skateboard rolls near. The scent gives them both a slight headache.

They touch, again; but this time her fingers are cooling – fast cooling.

The shadow of Arrow's skateboard rattles down the street, and then clatters past the car. Strange angles against the moon. His hand slaps their side mirror. Like he has thirteen fingers. Slam. It bounces off, hits the street but doesn't break. Stops. Reflects the light.

With relief the lover has something to say, hoping there'll be no fight.

"Look at that! Holy Shit! Did you see that kid! What a night! Little fucker got my mirror."

The skateboard's rumble is swallowed by the water's groan and roar. Our lover turns and tries to kiss some more. Hits a cheek. Her head's turning away. She lights a smoke.

Somehow, the vanilla smells stronger. He makes a joke about waiting for a smoke until "afterwards."

All he gets are frosted eyes, a plume of smoke that goes up his nose. "Let's try that engine again," she recommends, "better yet: let's not be lovers, not even friends. I'll make it clear – there ain't goin' to be no 'afterwards.'

Oh yeah. Vanilla makes me want to puke."

Our thwarted lover cranks the window down & holds his open hand against the chill, feels where the mirror used to be & remembers the boy's shadow on the reflected moon. Until Cascade Locks becomes still. Silence spills enters the earth and starts to grow.

Arrow has left the bow.

The Second Grain of Rice

Chem-trails settle into snow-burning, sticky, lace doilies that swing from cats-cradle fingers of the mountain ridge. A boulder rolls. Sucked from a socket; plucked by a rogue whirlwind.

In a shower of pebbles & trees & twigs, it rolls: bounces to shatter on a cliff. Shivers shake long ropes of rock. The ropes of rock do cut (knife-thru-butter) directly into the center of the waterfall & are sucked by longitudinal-splashing into the mouth of the vortex & straw-sucked into pools beneath the waterfalls. Hissing, burning ghee-rock-ropes drop and coil, splashing next to a match-box-cover Sea Lion. The Sea Lion rolls & lunges away, following its head & eyes in a sideways, awkward, dive into the underwater flow. Its huge bulk is a cigar-box ballet spin. The cave's smells and sounds are a dumpster load of falling empty sardine cans. You put your left fin in, you pull the right fin out...

Water ropes become DNA in slo-mo animation; helix hokey-pokey dancing with its double in this other cave with its ceiling mirrors, mirrors on the walls, carpets made of mirrors. Sea lions bellow and shift; manic Sumo-wrestling-polka dancing sea-lions are crazy-glued to the rock floor. Hear and smell the music! Sea lions now do the hokey-pokey & raise their heads, fish scales on their lips, shingled chap-stick lips; waving sea-worm whiskers in the elemental dance – bellow and roll, roll and bellow.

Through the rain forest there are unseen creatures and, once in a while, the denting of a leafy patch; the imprint of a large splayed multi-toed foot. That print fades like shadows in Science-fair experiments. There's squealing and shrieking. Birds rise like time-lapse puffballs. Hills shake wind into the ocean.

When the sun sets it pulls a net of darkness behind & drags that stretchy grid through the forest, across the plains and over the moss-covered roofs of forgotten houses. Green is ferning its way up the walls of houses, expanding in lime-popsicle-hue along the evestroughs that hang crooked. Buckled, their metallic fingers poke into burst rain-barrels.

The green – the vivid green – sips moisture from the sky; drinks up dusk.

The moon rolls large; a peregrine moon.

Craters pour their deep-blue blackness, cream-topped shadows skate along overtaken streets. Webs spun on old street lights now glisten as they hold moon droplets.

The central square with its mushroom-shaped oven waits.

All is waiting. The town's mouth yawns to the sky. Teeth are candy-crunch waiting.

Waiting.

The tides await.

The Cave shifts to the center of the circle. A storyteller is singing. There's the sound of music from a saw.

The center of a whirling spin-top of water is spun by moon-string tugged by lunar fingers. See it rise, tipped and spinning from the sea – growing in the salty hands of ocean-potters. A disk of water is cooking in the spray-foam-oven. A disk of water dented with the marks of lunar fingers. Spray is flying; lingering in moonlit glow.

See it tilt, tilt, tilt & level again, dragging the light of night deep into the ocean. Racing over the ocean is a spin-spun-top on a mirror. As it spins it grows dust devils on dead salt lakes lit by the pulsing sign of a cheap moonlit motel.

Moonlight is just a shave away from full moon in Pisces. Before this we are void of course. Nothing is as nothing does. We spin at an odd angle, like faulty mail-order trance-disks turned by the grip of inept hypnotists.

Underwater phosphoresce swirls back & forth and back & forth in systolic/diastolic beats that tighten your left arm in a blood pressure cuff of water and release it. The water twirls a dying dial.

As above and so below. So it goes; so it goes.

Below & above, above & below, swinging up & swinging down. Moving at first towards and, next, away from the hidden motel. Base rumblings pumping loud. When clouds begin to vibrate, and snow sparkles on the peaks – those peaks release the flakes. Snowflakes fall like a fluffed feather duvet with beaten mattress feathers: a pillow fight in a silent movie moving across the lens of our eyes. Eyes squint in the blinking headlights of roller coasters in the powdered sugar drift. Up and down. Blinking away the feathers. And the snow grows deep.

Wind blows flurries back to the mountains. Louder and louder, it makes mock of the philosophers' question of sound in the empty forest. The falling trees, the waves, the breeze, wind, the B-A-M of the falling water, *we all fall down!*

Oh yes we do & tumble in the sound. The maw of the water drinks salt water like Tao Master Lo drinking a big bowl of soup; slurping/slurping/slurping. The disk of water slurps up fish & spews them back again. This sound exists without needing any ears. Even eyes hook echoes from eye-fish books & hooks the letters of rocks that bounce & rise from hidden caves of sand. Pebbles tumble, tumble, tumble in Mother Nature's famous underwater-gem-polisher - like the one in my head. Tumbler fingers of butter now juggling flame are illuminating the mask of a butter-juggling master of ceremonies – that Juggler.

That sound! The sound that throws words into a book-binder shaking them round the eardrums of the hidden ear.

That sound travels past this book

You set it down by a bedside lamp before the alarm is clicked on. Perhaps, just before the alarm is clicked off.

Tick. Tick. Tick.

The whirlpool forms and reforms again & all our bookmarks are lost.

Pages flattened with steam do hiss in a magic city. Booklice run away.

All this we hear inside the cave. And we cuddle closer around the fire. Warm as it is, it pumps so much smoke that we cannot see each other.

Now I have learned to hold a sharpened quill in my tiny hand & before me, through two polished Coke bottle bottoms, I see the grain of rice as large as the die of a house. The letters that pump their way through my veins flow into my fingers, and each morning the old storyteller takes a metal-spring-loaded blood-pricker & pin-pricking cylinder & holds it against my finger, and click- in slo-mo - the point slams into my skin and through & when my seven year old finger is squeezed, drops of blood go down the quill to the sharpened point & I write what I hear whispered into my ears.

My eyes water and when they do, an old hand bathes my eyes. And all day, all night, I write and turn.

Click & write. Click & write. The new grain of rice turns with me, and crimson letters form.

I sit in a red chair. I am in the cave.

I am an old man striding through the woods.

I live upon the moon and play with glassine critters.

On earth, I die upon an isthmus.

On Mars, I live on a mountain.

Here? I am a headless shadow.

O!

Eve:

Eve's sleep prepares to unstick her
(the Velcroed writer)
from the smoggy fur
of one Los Angeles night.

Follow our trail of moonlight to a rumpled bed in Los Angeles where, tossing on a futon, the former queen-of-scripts is sleeping. Her veins contain flooding Prozac mixed with Gingko, Kava Kava, a splash of Vodka, a trace of weed & the banana-flavored frosting from a late night Winchell's doughnut.

At midnight, a raven sitting on the doughnut shop's lamp post looks at her & says quite clearly, "In writing there's no law!"

The raven pauses a moment, skips any reference to "Nevermore," and goes directly to a more banal yet resonating, "Caw." Eve wonders if the raven's real – if she, herself, is real. This becomes a puzzle she chooses to ignore. Turning her back on the raven, she'd headed home with donut sugar on her lips.

Eve's eyes are masked; her ears buckled by old-school Walkman earphones. In an earlier morning of this day she'd decided not to knuckle to the latest demands to change her much-changed script but, by late morning she'd forgotten that decision.

She crawled into a bed of chemicals to ease her pain, to help her pretend she might write again. About her scripts, she'd said "My moving finger is uplifted, and having writ...not all thy piety or wit can.. ah... make me turn this gold to shit...something…something..something or another...ah…erase a jot or....something. When do you need it?"

Perplexed; she could not recall the stanzas. Her previous photographic memory has clouds across the over-exposed film of it. Her brain is dull – no longer full of everything she's seen or heard since her memory first kicked in. It seems absurd that she'd forget something as simple as a word.

Her earphones, tinny in the pillows & buried inside the sweaty billows of a once-clean duvet, leak out a thin version of *Charity's Song*. Day has whirled by night, marched up the driveway & still in bed she lies. She suspects this new morning will arrive much too soon for her taste. Her brows are wrinkled with smoker's erosion much like sections of beach near Malibu where storm sewers stream over sand into a murky ocean, tearing at the sparse grass sprinkling the beach. "This will not do," she murmurs, falling into the sweaty arms of fitful sleep.

"I tell you. This will not do! I want my dreams!"

Television continues to play in Eve's room. Pale light spills across her face & she's covered in phosphorescent pixels from her only constant lover's high-def screen. Around her pillow there blows a Zen snowstorm of white paper sheets with black scratches all torn, scattered, & crumpled. Her bed-covering is black and Eve tosses on her back in the middle of this paper storm, falling towards sleep. Random pixels stamp across her sleep mask. Suddenly between thoughts, she has the ending, beginning & most of the middle of her script.

Eve wants to get up, tries to loosen the grip of sleep, worries about money just to wake herself up, but no such luck. She falls off her mind in a skidding plunge, feels her legs twitch and jump, her hands grasp at the falling sheets. Too late! Her body shudders, dissolves, lunges, melts – an ice-candle in the stream of sleep.

Her rumpled night-dress bunches near her waist, her sleeping mask goes crooked & her first dream smears images of film-bosses in thin greasy trails across her brain.

They shout at her – "In tinsel-town, you'll never work again. By the way, who was supposed to pay for lunch?"

Go closer now. See a swollen pulse beating time on each side of her temple. Her graying touched-up hair is streaked & modified through habit; no longer with hopes of attracting youthful desire. Nonetheless, her veins still pulse-pulse. See those lifting veins of her temples throb & shift like threadbare hoses at a three alarm fire.

Go closer now, past the tangled nest where she's stopped plucking her eyebrows. "I could shave them off and burn them out for you and tattoo fake ones on & you'll never have to pluck again" offered Bob, an artist friend of hers who once tattooed, according to him, Johnny Depp & claimed he'd crafted a blue anchor on the left fetlock of Mr. Ed. That was before the end of all her friendships with artists, writers, actors, assorted freaks – the time when she'd started to forget who'd shared her bed and body.

Now instead of enjoying boozy sleep-overs, her various rebuffed & forgotten former lovers do sulk & hang out in bars discussing how Eve's once-clever mind has gone to join her vanished body. This was the time where she stopped returning phone calls; first for weeks, then months, then years & now, well, not ever.

Go closer: in the center of her forehead is a reflected patch of light rippling. The shot inside the TV screen changes from dark to light & back through light to dark again, sliding across darker nipples, to pool in shadows in the night.

"There's something gone wrong with her brain," her agent offers as an excuse when phoned, trying to explain why Eve's late with scripts again & still again. His explanation does not halt Eve's fall from grace. And when she falls from grace, she leaves executive memory without a trace, less than the sinking of a rock in outer space.

Behold her mouth and her lips drawn back over perfect teeth, television blinking in reflection from her bleached incisors. Behold the crow's feet at the corner of her eyes and lips – her once-full lips. The lipstick smear on her teeth shines purple in the glow of the box that's set into the corner.

Eve speaks again, tossing in sweat. The glare washes her in odd color: "I'm here! I'm finally here."

The lights brown-out & she is spinning, a spiral in the night.

Falling into the last emotion left for her that is totally unfiltered and real – she feels fright.

Moonlight is in the cave. The fire banked, the storyteller sleeps. Even the cauldron simmers in sleep.

Occasionally, something floats to the surface. Sometimes a sinking yacht rises only to sink again. Other times a tropical island surfaces, and Bob Marley sings, and his words mantle the sleeping children, and their smiles move in rhythm to the reggae, and then the Island sings & sinks.

The liquid burbles & we see Crete sifting its beaches to the edges of the kettle, and Ravens leaving the beaches. Wings beating, they tear from the surface, and circle the cave, rising to the smoke hole spilling clouds with helicopter prop-wash. Shadows wash the floor of the cave. *Don't worry about a thing*...beat, beat, beat, more Rasta beats over the sleepers. Their fingers tapping, feet moving. In dreams they dance. All across the isthmus, each dancing with a quill in either hand.

'I am a writer,' thinks each.

'I write with my skateboard, my pen, my lovers, my sidewalks, my memories of a man of a midnight jacket.

I write with raven feathers'.

The Ravens do float down gifts before they leave. Each one drops two wing feathers, one left, one right.

Seven Ravens drop fourteen feathers. Each child, head still forming, uncurls their hands, and when they awaken they find a feather in each hand, a deep pot of soot-forged ink.

But now, the dying flames flutter across their faces. All mirrors are removed.

The face of the cave sees the seven ravens fly towards the motel, descending past the Easter Island statues rising from dark loam in the courtyard.

The statues lean ahead. They rise higher, revealing white cloth shoulders.

Their heads tilt upwards, watching the seven Ravens circle in descent.

The Music Girl:

The Music Girl sits at a piano
in Vermont & plays pure beauty,
never daunted by her life.

The hall where the Music Girl plays is haunted, but she's not scared by ghosts. She knows that Spirits like to hear her music. It opens hidden doorways & helps them journey between worlds.

When she sits at the piano, ghosts draw near from the Plainsfield fields, from the Vermont forest, from Aspen groves that tremolo-sing from the upper & the lower gardens where Susannah Martin was removed & imprisoned & then hanged as a witch in sixteen-hundred-and-ninety-two. Now, back as a spirit in the garden, Susannah guards (with the moon) those who hold music in their hearts; those who know the spilling of words from the eyes and down the cheeks. This ghost knows and protects, from the mighty, the meek. Amongst them, is the Music Girl.

The Music Girl prefers as an audience, the forest, stream, and field ghosts to the dense slow moving real-life spirits haunting her at home. Those real-life ghosts are called, by neighbors, 'parents'.

This night the Music Girl greets the wind; welcomes the small lights in tree branches; plays to the glow in brambles where flying light & shadow makes her laugh at the tickle in her lungs and mind. These lights & spirits are more a family than her kith & kin. Her link is not a skin-deep text-book description of DNA's slim strands. Her strands are infinite, lasting longer than the stars. One day her music will travel far to reach those she has, up to this sweet night, seen in a land glimpsed only in her deepest reverie.

Tonight her house is too warm to hold her. Her parents are giants. Faces smeared with fried chicken, they drop bones to the floor while they chew meat as if it's bubble-gum. They are so dense, so larded in their bodies, that the furniture becomes ethereal – composed of refracted lights created by various Elves, Faeries, Pixies, Gnomes, Sprites who hitch rides with fast-food delivery trucks.

The Music Girl walks towards the Haybarn Hall through shadowed forest. She watches a full moon pouring time like buttermilk light. The night begins to ring with delicate winter chimes.

Her heart soars into the moon's eyes; falls upwards through the sky; is enclosed in the folded shawl of a moon-being, of an ancient woman wrapped in a blue shawl – a crone who holds the Music Girl's heart, rejecting nothing & blessing all. This ancient woman stares out of her night eyes; pale yellow heart beating as sure and true as the center of the moon. The Music Girl holds her hands towards those lunar eyes & laces her fingers with Grandmother-in-the-moon's. She feels fingers lacing back. A crackle of moonlight ripples over the crescent moons of her finger nails. This land in Vermont, this magical country in the forest, sways & whips with wind – her hands are spread in light against the moon.

At home she's known as the quiet girl.

Never a word to her parents.

She sometimes slips between them and their television & when their heads bob to either side of her they ask if she wants to stay and watch reruns with them. Saying nothing she bows, as an acolyte may bow under a vow of silence & leaves the room without a word. Her parents bob back to center, bathed in the holy light of television. Watching commercials, they laugh and talk while mounds of chicken bones pile up beside their twin La-z-Boys. Sometime, there's a pause in what the television is saying & they use this pause to talk of their quiet daughter, of how she never says a word. The TV continues to prattle. They text other viewers.

Sometimes people are killed in various shows & there's war news, abduction news, election news, birds fall from the skies, cows tip over and die in distant fields, dead seals wash up on the shores of Newfoundland. People hate America. People in America hate people who hate America. Neutrals hate both. When they're not talking they kill each other. Sometimes they vote, sometimes they're deposed. Mostly they sleep poorly at night and can't quite figure why. Even the end of the world won't stop the talking. Voices travel laborious trajectories. The television talks and broadcasts. Right to the edge of this Universe. Everything is explained. Politics goes on forever: this one in and that one out while voters are lost at sea. Sometimes there are reality shows about moneyed strangers. Just when you think the crooks are gone, they get voted back by those they robbed before. "Welcome back, we've left an open door."

Late night, there's enough blood and flesh to keep people watching. Women die in various ways on television, pleading for life. Her parents have come to believe that all they see is real.

"Jeez, I knew she'd die," says the father.

"Me too!" replies the mother.

And between the women with knives held to their throats, and scattered amongst people in swimsuits marooned on desert islands, in between televised dinner parties of former celebrities, & woven throughout programs filled with desperate eyes wanting fame, one War-Mart president replaced – hooray. Oh, oh he's coming back again as a concierge...oh, oh...here they come, boys & girls – all over the world here they come again with polyester hair and capped, tooth-whitened teeth. Stamp. Stamp. Bottom-line boys. Stamp. Stamp. Don't lift those hands too high. Stamp. Stamp. Firm handshakes, tired dull minds & here they come again. The hucksters are circling in DC, the hucksters are landing outside DC. 'Remember the boomerang,' is their favorite motto. Yep! God's in his big saddle. Yippee. They live inside their never ending news commercials where they sell selling; that place where they sell buying. Inside-the-box boys. Guts

No wonder the world always needs a mountain.

Her parents drink brand drinks and they eat brand snacks & they vote brand-name votes. In their driveway is a brand-name car. And they shake their heads at the TV news & they gasp at the latest kidnappings & shootings, for they believe, O, they *truly* believe in all they see. With every bite of chicken they believe and chomp. They wonder if their car could be adapted to run on chicken grease – just like them.

They smile and lean back, looking like rich tourists on warm sands of perfect beaches until the sky chills and drifts TV snow and they tug their sweaters around them with greasy hands and stop their words about their quiet daughter. No news of bad times reached them – they lost money in the way they lost memory. They didn't worry – they had High Definition. They didn't worry - they had PVR. No worries. "Hell with it," they say. "The hell with it."

The Music Girl enters the empty Haybarn theatre.

Waiting for her is a grand piano. Light & shadows await her fingers. Alone she sits at the keyboard until she hears the spirits enter. Before she plays she lingers; chanting prayers upon her lips.

"Let this my gift be free, let it show to those with open hearts, the heart of me. One day may what I play reach those who live on earth. Let it take them to the realms that Grandmother Moon knows, let it give birth to what they will become – each and every one. Let my music blow through their hearts like a fierce wind that tumbles them and their hearts to the place where flows the stream, let them learn to take and turn inside-out their dreams."

A soft wind against a curtain her music spreads, ripples, drifts outside, touching spirits. It rustles leaves, patterns streams & Aeolian-harps its zephyr through the hearts of all of us who gather in our sleep.

Something is cooking in the cave.

The storyteller stirs the pot again and, once in a while, more odd objects float to the top. When the fire cracks its knuckles, sparks do fly upwards through the smoke, and fall back again where they turn to soot.

On their way down each becomes a spark of light & shadows swing back & forth like snaking fronds of a subterranean carwash.

Sometimes the teller of tales is an old man, other times an old woman. Sometimes both combine, with four arms stirring. That's the one our circle likes the most, but we never say so – scared it will go away.

This time the storyteller's robes look blue, deep blue like water that a blade churns up from the Atlantic ocean in the middle of a storm – so blue 'tis almost slate. A woman this time, she stirs the cauldron with an oar, and I'm drawn closer and closer – not only by the smell of soup, but by the smudge of smoke, as if I'm being charcoaled against the inner whiteness of the robe, bezeled by the demarcating line against the blurring white. It's got the depth of a piece of coal that's been worked like beach glass on a rocky beach.

I draw closer, as do all the others in my group. The smoke deepens and shifts, so every time I believe I see a face, just when I almost guess who's there with me, their image vanishes into soot, or is blink-dazzled so bright that I must close my eyes. The only place to rest my sight is when I look onto the surface of the soup.

It shifts, and on the churning paddle, a skateboard forms, and drips along the oar. The soup turns red, the oar goes black. I move so close that I see a face.

Arrow:

Highway skateboard singing blues and red,
Arrow sails, and naps in asphalt's bed.

It takes a while for Arrow to find a truck that matches his style of hooking rides. That truck needs to have an outcropped bumper & mirrors placed so a blind spot covers what he does outside when gliding from the shadows of the road to grab the strut above the doors, secure a slim cord that hooks into the struts, pay the line out, wiggle into balance on the upward slope, looking like a jumping salmon on a rope behind the truck.

His luck holds.

The truck grinds through early gears and Arrow feels little fear, having done this so often he always knows when he's struck gold. He looks like a water skier; night-dust flutters gray-feather plumes behind the wooden bar that he grips, the bar he fashioned from his mother's left-behind broom (given to her on her wedding day by a former lover who, hearing of that wedding, went away).

The truck staggers into third, tugging Arrow behind it. Speed begins to mount. The resurfaced road is smooth. Skateboard wheels knock, then hum. The rope being new, tightens and twangs like virtuoso slides on steel guitars. At sixty miles an hour Arrow's thin dreadlocks thrum, standing straight out behind him just behind the truck. He senses his grip is good & when the Semi crests the ridge he stands up from his crouch just as the rear-view mirrors show a receding view of Cascade Locks.

Arrow releases the rope. A Canada Goose set loose from the flock, he veers to the wrong side of the road. For seconds – side by side – the boy and mighty truck keep pace. The joy of this keeps Arrow flying straight as his name. He's thrilled the trucker doesn't notice him. No wonder, he's instead, listening to C & W music; raising a balding head up to the moon – trying to sing along with Country tunes, knowing that someday he'll sing in Nashville his fame sure to spread as he's introduced to the Grand Ole Opry as the "*Lonesome Trucker*" or the "*Singing Canadian Goose.*" The driver bows in his mind and smiles.

"A perfect night. I have escaped the Locks," yells Arrow to the moonlit clouds.

A CB unit inside the truck hisses and coughs and squeaks along. A voice, filled with static is high-pitched with urgency. The roar of the truck & singing wheels conceals the content from Arrow, which is a shame because the words would save him from what will maim and batter; that shatters him, smashing the portals of his brain.

The CB unit crackles and bursts with static again & a voice yells "....this asshole...*hiss*...driving... in...*crackle*...

night...climbing hill... wrong side... no lights... hunch *...hiss ...* he's ... drunk *...crackle......hiss"*

The trucker clicks off Dwight Yokem in mid song, stamps on his hi-beams & for the first time looks left and sees the kid who's tagged along. A quick double take as he sees Arrow and signals frantically for the kid to pull over – to stop. But Arrow thinks the trucker is simply doing a grown-up thing & keeping his speed, he looks the panicked trucker in the eye, giving him the finger with a smile. Before the driver can think of what else to do to warn this skater there's a sudden cry of tires from the drunk's oncoming car skidding from the tarmac to the shoulder and back towards the center of the road. The trucker tugs the air horn to warn the boy and the oncoming drunk.

Arrow knows something is terribly wrong – he sees it in the trucker's eyes. Quickly, he shifts his view and looks ahead to see a beater; old V8 with lights shut off, glinting in the moonlight as it skids towards him up the hill. Arrow's traveling too fast to jump off – too late to shift his path.

What hits him is the grill; turning him like pizza dough, making all time stand still. The first thought in his mind – "Oh Fuck. I'm road kill!"

Each moment stretches a mile or two & up-and-down the hill, as Time-without-pain throws Arrow across the hood, his face a spout of blood – bones crunching slowly beneath the peeling skin, then back into the bounce again.

The car fishtails sideways, throwing Arrow in the air & with its headlights turned all-at-once-on, it tumbles into the chasm, light beams spinning until flame blasts the bottom of the gulch. There's a roar; the distant rain of falling glass. Arrow, flap-jacked into the sky, turns at the same time as the car. A steel puffball sends flying spores of flame towards the boy, this bone-curled-frozen-slinky boy hanging like a thawed pork chop in mid-air.

Arrow is silhouetted against the moon. His head leaks fluid, his skateboard travels on without him; clattering over the edge to join the dead guy in the car below. The Trucker jack-knifes his rig to a stop, just as Arrow leaves the moon and descends back to earth.

"Christ," – the driver thinks – as he runs towards the boy – "this kid looks like he's been run over by a train."

The trucker can feel no pulse, but he swears, as he leans nearer, that he can hear the kid cry. Leaning closer to the boy's lips, he hears him speak. He leans close enough to understand Arrow's words are only throat gurgles. The driver bows towards the moon and prays.

"No matter what it takes," – he pleads – "may this boy stay alive. No matter what it takes. If he dies here, I swear, I'll never drive again."

A cruiser squeals to a stop with its lights reflecting off Arrow's slippery skin. Truckers gather while Arrow gurgles.

"Jesus, was that sound from the kid?" asks one Police Officer the younger of the two and rushes off to hurl behind the cruiser.

The older officer, nodding, adds: "There's no way this boy will last the night."

Somewhere inside the shattered mess, Arrow hears what was said & takes a silent oath that he will not be dead meat. Somehow, no matter what it takes, he will live.

You're making a mistake" says the trucker to the cop, "This kid has what it takes. He'll live beyond the night. He's got fight."

No one else believes the trucker except Grandmother-the-moon who bathes Arrow's face with light, not minding blood or tears or gravel-in-the-flesh. She's seen wars and bombings & torture & people falling from great heights; she has observed wings smoking against the sky, lighting up a dark moon night. People fall off cliffs and read maps, people fall out of skyscrapers and bounce off awnings to walk away. Grandmother Moon knows what punishment a strong heart may take and yet not die.

See Arrow – his eyes half open.

See the moon's reflection in the cop's eyes.

See the moon pulsing the night.

Arrow tries to tell all who have gathered, something … anything... to sing a small tune through puddling blood. His gurgling brings shivers to the gathered men. And then pure light begins to surround him. His breathing becomes shallow & still the great light beats. His song is hidden in his lungs he loses consciousness and all his being can do as light unfurls is bear the fire of pain now moving through him - feel healing pain - feel stay-alive pain.

All he can do is, rapidly, shallowly, try his best not to leave this world.

Queen Mab:

A strange hall for others does not her disturb,

she knows that fate brought her to this place
– not to be a noun – but to live inside a changing verb.

"Mab," says the nurse at admitting, "Why, that's a pretty name."

Mab nods & sighs & smiles; happy to have this old-memory moniker back in her head for a while, feeling some cogs of recall creaking and turning. Better than being called "Professor."

Her feet are damp.

"My name's Yemaya. You're Mab?"

"Queen Mab... " she shouts back (although she did not mean to shout) "...I am."

She drops her voice to a stentorian gale, the whisper of a whale, "... Queen Mab."

Stephen Lo, the crisp-as-starched-linen-napkins orderly, grandson of Skipper Lo himself, gives a sweeping bow when she adds, "I, Queen Mab of the Faeries, bear no malice."

Stephen smiles and bows again. " Ah. The Faeries? Then you can't be all bad if you're the queen of such fine folk."

He and the Nurse smile. They have, towards Queen Mab, no malice and feel no rush a'tall to admit her on this slow night despite the fullness of the moon. The wind rises – blowing towards the door, rattling Venetian blinds, clanging empty tin cans into one thin chain of sound. It shivers Mab.

"What's bad?" asks Mab. "Has something here gone bad? Is there a problem with those left alone in my palace?"

She's scared, caged wolf scared – unable to turn around.

"I was a professor of ... something, before I became Queen Mab."

Yemaya and Stephen glance at each other. Neither of them believe in CAT Scans or tests of reciting numbers backwards from sixty to one. What they see in Mab is not filtered by a series of tests. They watch the fright in her eyes – as she forgets all she has said so far this night. The big fluorescent's behind her, and all around her are other small lights. Along her shoulder, near her ears, are spherical lights, one over each eyebrow. "Looks like glitter" thinks Stephen. But when he leans closer to look, each light blinks out. When he leans back from her, they blink on again. "Must be late nights," he thinks, "must be the rain caught in her hair."

She leans ahead, caught in image by the convex mirror, but the faded, mercury all gone, section of the mirror is exactly where her head is placed. So, above her shoulders there's only mist. Mist and small blinking lights. Stephen makes a move as delicate as falling lace moves (gentle to the eyes of Mab is this undisturbing-of-her-space move.)

"Here let me show you to your new room and bed."

"It's not in the cellar is it?" asks Mab, "Not beneath the old floorboards?"

"No ma'am" he replies, "it's on the very highest floor that this hospital has."

"Hospital! Why am I in a hospital? I do not want to be in a hospital. Don't you see? I'm an independent woman. Let me out!"

The Nurse, experienced with such fear, looks Mab directly in the eyes and moves near, placing her hand upon the arm of the Queen.

"This is just a stopover on your way to..."

"On my way to where?"

"Why" says Stephen, "This is your...palace."

Mab smiles a regal smile, "This is good." She draws a regal breath.

"It is the place you missed ...the place you choose, Queen Mab. This place may be anything you wish."

"Ah," says Mab, her regal manner now again in place.

"Please take me to the Throne Room, if you must, so I may once more sit with Elves and Faeries nine & Gnomes and Pixies. Where we may dine on mushrooms dusted with a little Pixie dust."

"Of course, your Majesty. Let's be off to the grand hall."

"I hope you don't find this a strange request?" For a moment, Mab puzzles about where she is, who these mysterious dressed-in-white people are.

"This request is not at all strange" answers Yemaya, "We've had many requests. Once an old farmer wanted to finish his time back on the range. Another time a former smoothie-maker wanted a simple concession stand in a strip mall. An old confidence man wanted to live inside a mola. He's still there, part of the shadow of a jaguar."

A pause.

"Some of our friends here play in the grid-bar."

"Grid-bar? What is a grid-bar?" wonders Mab to herself but does not ask aloud, in fear that she'd appear a fool for asking. So she remains mute. The way Queen Elizabeth might remain very still, plate untouched at a Rotary luncheon.

Yemaya continues, "Each writes their own world. Some of our guests run Karaoke bars. One is a Nun who knows the secret symbolism of Hildegard Von Bingham. Another lives outside in the yard, raising Tofu-chickens for the Dali Lama. Others are content to simply...sit around, heads bent, arms akimbo."

Mab nods her head; cups chin in hands, and whistles a scrap of a forgotten song.

Stephen the Orderly gently holds her by the elbow. "And now, your Majesty, it's time for you, although pressing matters of state may lie on your mind, to travel with me as I take you through the winding of the maze-like corridors of out-of-power people, the dispossessed of mind & those of us dispossessed by economic, racial, & cultural bias, yet predisposed to, without comment, assist you to find your great Mead-hall."

"Mead Hall?" asks Mab eyes wide, "Is that not the hall where night and death await those who have traveled too far too often alone, too late to arrive when others do?"

And then she forgets her train of thought. She pauses.

"What is this place?"

"It is not what it seems" replies Yemaya "For you, perhaps, it Paradise may be?"

"If the spell's gone away, why then, we'll see..." says Mab. "But I must be borne as a Queen is borne to her hall in chariot. With footmen, attendants & all their retinue."

Stephen bows to sounds of invisible lace, a glimpse of past-life brocaded stockings, "Perhaps this will do, to bear you to your hall in my chariot of aluminum wheels."

"What are your names, my friends?"

Bowing, crisp, attendant, all in whites: "I am Stephen Lo. 'Neck of the Bellows;' my uncle is old Skipper Lo, my lineage. If you want the source."

Smiling, with folded smoky arms: "I am Yemaya. 'Ocean Goddess' if you want the source. Lakes, if there's no ocean."

Regal is Mab's look as she shifts into the wheel chair & royal is the bow, once more, of the best orderly on this forgotten floor. The wheelchair rolls on velvet wheels, deep inside Mab's mind.

When she departs, Yemaya shakes her head.

"I wonder" she muses "just what this Queen will find."

<u>Arrow:</u>

His brain still lives,
helped by machines' whirls.
Arrow hangs suspended
between two equal worlds.

Where is he, this boy, while doctors work on his brain? The Darth-Vader-breaths that he takes; his mummer-like, in-and-out-panting makes nurses and doctors shudder again and again. The color of the antiseptic - green cloth against reddish brown stains - a cold black-widow spider, metallic thin, holding skull flaps pulled back – pinned; Arrow has remaining flaps of his skull, pinned.

His feet, scraped and peeled, point upwards, his remaining toes are cramped & bunched as he holds on to the spinning earth in one position with his feet. Ceiling & floor do the blender-spin around him. His spine is the pin. He holds all, sees all, hears all; each voice a time-lapse sonic flower in the din. He hears small hooves in a cave.

In all the instruments' bleatings; the din of sharp and clanging sounds surrounding him; the hum of electronics, the smell of cauterizing, the chat of the O.R. Doctor about her weekend, of her abandoned hopes of being once more an imperfect bride (not by way Frankenstein but of Harvard and other fine schools) and enjoying a man of blood, of excessively beating flesh – oh yes, and a well-tuned brain. She speaks of her lost weekend's plans; of her attempts to unsuccessfully find even an imperfect man, someone who's kind and fun – someone totally different than … well, the previous one!

Then there is the volunteering of the anesthetist Dr. Boyle to become her very imperfect man. Lights bounce off his buckled dome. A dent delivered by a Celtic assailant in a time-distant Dublin bar, remains in the center of his head – the souvenir of a bouncing, ricocheting pint. That kind of student night. He didn't know the dent would be permanent until years went along with his departing hair & his old mother stared at the emerging canyon of the dent.

"Like a meteor hit Madame Tussaud's skull" she laughed.

Deciding it was the necessary time, Dr. Boyle moved to America.

Laughter mixes deep inside the Operating Room music.

Rock and roll does ebb & flow, a living breathing working noise. Where in all this cacophony may we find what is left of Arrow? This boy, set down upon a cold hard metal table, is living somewhere inside the pulsing of his damaged smeared-in-sections brain & his compressed, pork-pull, torn body.

Where is our hidden boy?

Arrow still flies on his skateboard through the shawl of the full moon. He touches, without fear, the face of Grandmother Moon and stretches his arms into the black sky so he may pour stars through his fingers. Mars planet-punches all the way through ear lobes, leaving behind its rounded blood-dot-sparkles.

He does a half-pipe, sliding down and up the Milky way, spinning round so fast his words fray & tatter. When he tries to whoop, his feet, beneath the green cloth, twitch & his memory becomes an itch behind what used to be his mind. The sounds and sights from the brief history of his life go spinning as he blurs into the black pixel-points of outer and of inner space. Expanding, he hears a chanting echo. If he had any words left he would throw them like dice down the wishing well of his mind. Clatter, clatter, splash.

All words of his own are gone, leaving room for a song of empty space to pour into him, to fill him with emptiness to the brim and over the rim of the operating room.

This song unlocks him, raises a deeper gate of his mind, flooding to a new level, washing and filling with starlight. The song is of the stars mixed with the doc, singing along with the O.R. nurses (a Dar Williams tune about Christians and Pagans). The rolling of the moon rounds out the song. Cheeps and bleats and static and hums, words of "This kid almost bought it." All this expands through all empty spaces.

The words of Dr. Boyle enter a sudden quiet place.

"Might have been better if he'd died with his mind burning like a light. Ringing like a silver dollar on a mahogany bar."

There's a pause; a mopping-up of truth from the floor. No one bothers to disagree. Some gossip joins the closing of the spread-apart head, the rapid suturing of the wound; the cutting of old-fashioned stitches, the removing of the gloves, the wheeling of Arrow to the first of many different beds.

While he sleeps, his mind tries to find his missing skateboard. Locates it near Orion's belt & finds he's clothed in fox-fur pelts, his hair intertwined with feathers of a speckled swan that's sailing on the deep lake of *Mare Tranquilitas*. All memories erased, he tumbles in infinite embrace. Arrow has gone so far that his skateboard may never return.

He joins together, point by point, the stars & then, greeted by inner night he expands, feeling his heart soar.

Arrow becomes many huge, red, beating lights – pulling softly over his head a blanket made of pebbled night pinned into place by warm pulsing lights.

I fall asleep not knowing who I am.
  I awaken as a girl.
My fingers touch my lips, and I whisper to myself.
I am here, I am in a cave, and I am a boy.
I am here, I am in a cave, and I am a girl.
The fire rustles, the soup remaining in the pot comes to a boil again, and some water hisses to the flame below.
It shifts thru steam to smoke again. I hear the oar being dipped, turning. And in the steam-smoke, lit from behind, I see my shoes.

Eve:

Falling through her 'nothing-like-Hollywood'
dream, into a life with no sighs of 'should'
or 'must,' she feels her brain shed rust
as she spins and dances, while on fire.

Her writing, though once admired
Is now, with great energy, discussed
& the conclusion is that, a Madame Tussaud writer,
she and her words cover dents with a patina of dust.

Eve's feet rest on black leather.

Her left shoe is red, her right shoe black, her dress has become dusty purple. By her side, a box of Kleenex.

In the window appears, reflected from a mirror in the corner, an image in a triple glazed window of a fifty minute clock. Hands don't move until they zoom. The kind of clock issued only to therapists.

She stops to breathe, to cross her feet and finally, after thirty minutes silence of her fifty-allotted-minutes, to begin to talk.

"In the dream it's always the same. I'm standing on a deeply wooded slope, overlooking a small town. It's almost midnight, full moon pushing against the details of what I see, small white houses, with brightly colored roofs picket fences and a strange geodesic dome in the center of this place. I feel profoundly lonely & no matter where I stare, there are no familiar faces.

Wait, let me remember… In this night I see no people anywhere. Strong winds sprinkle leaves across me; unseen fingernails tickle my skull. The moon sends shadows running from house to house. As fast as I run, they run with me. Shadows from childhood, from failed marriages, from studio executives and bill collectors. I'm more like these running shades, than I am like real people. The darker it grows in this world, the more begins to happen. Even though I can't see any people in the sleep-built town, lights build into a glow inside the houses.

No harsh clicks of electric lights switching on. Instead, there's a warm glimmer of lamplight blurring darkness pouring out the windows to lie upon fresh snow-drifts like shadowed tea-stains on once-white, once-bright, ironed & creased linen tablecloths. When the wind blows snow around my shoulders, it forms a white shawl. I don't feel the cold. You know how it is when you empty a toaster oven? Remember? The dark crunch of the brown crumbs, warm if you've just made toast? That's how the snow falls in my dream, and it crunches too.

My time is up? Oh. Fifty minutes gone?

Just like that?

No. I won't come back. No more appointments needed. I'll talk to my journal.

Journal?

The one inside my head.

Yeah, that's what I said – the one inside my head. You can bill the guild. I'm sure you can work it out. Good bye, my old trout. I'd rather talk to my journal than a shrink. I can spill ink in my journal."

Eve's Journal:

Inside my head. Where Studio Executives dread to go: PRIVATE! IF YOU READ THIS I MEAN *YOU*. Oh what the fuck – read!

Is this how it works
the great forgetting of how things end?
The books I read
the lines of a simple poem
all faded no longer near
&
the tip of my tongue
no longer near
my easy reach into memory's pantry
where I could reach with assurance
for the few things I knew.

Memory always worked for me before
Whispering where I'd placed
my bottle of wine upon a worn
cigarette scarred table.

And I could while sucking down smoke
reach without looking
to pick it up and pour it out.

No more.

The tip of the iceberg
in my mind is now just that:
with everything I knew
submerged
in a deep sea of books and images
from other people's art.

Perhaps from other people's hearts
and minds all now forgotten.
Is this how it works
the heart forgetting,

after a skip or two
to beat?

Eve's Journal Of Dreams:

(This is where I hold my dreams in letters of twine to tie them down so when I come back to these twine-tied pages I may then read them. These letters are now my memory: twine-tying memory.)

"Because the night gets darker and darker; dark as the center of a hidden core, I can see fingerprinted whorls of paint and grain. Long splinters in the picket fences rise against the moon, middens on a sharp ninety degree mountain, old stick trees in forgotten forests. Dead. I understand that (perhaps for the first time in my life) following the harmonic song of an unseen chorus, I've come home.

This is a new feeling and my heart begins to hurt with the newness of it. The hurt grows and grows & my chest starts to burn, a fire that I can't put out. I brush my breasts, trying to extinguish the flames. O... so true... so true, fingers on fire burning like the fires of Harbour Grace.

My fingers ignite orange dead boughs that are falling, spreading sparks as they tumble down, allowing fire to leap from my burning hands to cross the town & licking picket fences. Flames crawl along clapboard, leak under doors & window sashes to make lamps inside the homes explode in gashes of orange, and deep vermilion splash. Sending burning lamp oil into the world.

Hear timber crashing into living rooms. See flaring lintel & sash suck in the strangled breath and glare of burning pipe organs, accordions, fiddles & red hot saws. Flames singe music & music sparks from the front yards into the dark sky. Sky spreads color like the opened belly of a young, thrashing salmon on snow.

Snow catches on fire & everything in me wants to sing but my throat and tongue feel charred, & ashes grit my teeth before the desire to sing bursts fire.

The snow keeps notes from forming. I'm not a crying person and, at the same time, I'm not known as a woman who's in control of her life. I do lose control, but I don't cry – ever. So, for me to wake up this morning with tears pouring down my face like a river nearing the sea is a feeling so bleak for me that I wonder if any person anywhere in the world can feel like this get up and face the day. But I do.

Early morning. I know the sun is outside somewhere but the valley is brownish yellow, with the sky glowing from outside & painted in deep oils by Turner. This morning, after fighting my way out of the tangled covers, I run from the bedroom as if the bed's on fire. When I see the smog that smudges Hollywood's dome roll past my plate glass window there might as well be a fire inside my chest.

I continue running naked down the street & am suddenly (where does the dream end & where does the dream start?) on Mulholland running and running. Is this a dream -?- horns blowing! I run and run and this is real. Is this a dream? Asphalt on my bare feet is melting tar. The air smells smoky and gritty no longer and the smell of the sharp tack of antiseptic grows stronger & stronger and those who scorn me and my work are far behind. I run. I run some more. This is more than a fifty minute dream.

I have lost my way & am dropping words behind me as I run and run and…

…A totally naked woman with her mid-life breasts almost-synchronized in their bouncing; flesh shifting eyes wide open in daytime dreams, I think of what to say and unable to find a sentence, I draw in my breath, I let it burst out in a scream. Then all is still.

Discarded beside the roadside is a tattered blanket that I wrap around my body. The ecstasy is gone leaving a small still point – beacon on a fearsome night. It blinks and winks above my house as if the whole city is no longer ignoring what I do.

I turn and walk, my blanket tight about me. I head towards my now intensely strange Hollywood home.

I wonder what's next. "

An empty wind blows along the halls of the old motel. Empty until one scrap of paper is caught by each zephyr's hands, then folded & slipped under a door.

When it appears in the room, it unfolds – a simple message is left at the step into the jungle hut growing from sand on the floor:

In the misty island of Newfoundland, an old woman dreams.
Maud Tilley's white hair drifts across flour-sack pillow cases.
She's part of the bed; the bed part of her. When she in-breathes, the

room trembles. When she out-breathes, the room expands and glows.

Pink blotches on her cheeks match embroidered carnations on the white cloth. A crow flies overhead – dips a wing and feels the black air. Seeing the old woman's dreams seep through the ceiling, the crow banks left and heads towards the moon.

Maud's dream is as wide as her arms. Spreading her ancient elbows to hold the night sky, she rolls over on her back. Arms wide, her outstretched fingers are tickled by distant receding stars.

Her eyelids nova, revealing a couple of spinning galaxies. Maud's lids blink shut again. Slowly, lips open, old crooked teeth bite the morning light.

"I am the stars."

-Blink-

…and all begins again
&
again
&
again.

In other rooms, drooping aqua-tinted wallpaper with silver streaks once again rises & sticks re-pasted against the wall. This time the paste holds. Paper glows. The old shag carpet is once again that popsicle shade of psychedelic lime: the bed floats one more time, just centimeters above the floor. As if in an earthquake, the floor ripples & walls do the heart-beat of boom-boom::boom-boom: paintings appear from space and hang on nails that are, of a sudden, in the wall.

The corridors are filling with creatures from Easter Island, and as they open the doors to the less-than great outdoors, the snow blows in. The Easter Islanders shuffle thru the hallways. Buckets of black sticks are thrown and adhere to the walls in hexagrams 12 & 11. Their concave eyes are shadows eating pumice, and their hands, moving in awkward asbestos gloves, lift more coal-black I-Ching sticks & place them parallel outside each door. Snow drifts pupils slit-crossing their shadowed & pumiced eyes.

In the cave, the children circle the Storyteller. The cave kids hands raise Raven feathers that flutter as they run round and round. The cauldron lifts, as if it's filled with helium instead of the stuff of the world.

Higher. Higher.

As it gains height, the cauldron begins to turn, spinning one direction, while the children spin in the other. Now each sees the other's face – one another's eyes.

Widershins. Clockwise.

Clockwise. Widershins.

Water cuts around the slim beach.

The children rise, lifting from the heavy sandy floor a necessary quilt. Their hands gripping pumice feathers. On the floor the sand is multi-colored, faint pink, green, blue, yellow, an unfinished curve near the walls. The children float upwards with the smoke.

Finally, think they all, we may fly.

Finally, we may become our stories.

Inside the Motel, there's an island hut. Deep inside one of the motel rooms it has settled. In that room is the beach of Zeno & the Easter Island Beings go in & their magnetic hands hover above the sand that covers the lime-green shag carpet. The sand is as white as ashtray sand, as deep as bitumen, as blue as my skin. It also begins to float. Vortexing, it circles in slow revolutions around its core & pours towards the courtyard.

Heat steams across the snow, stars fall, springtime leaves crinkle; far away, the cyclotron recycles. Scientists now time-lapse, looking at the skies, staring into the void, annotating & blogging, forming virtual astrobiological sites in India. White coats are drifting – snowy coats once again caught in an Eastern wind. Summertime steams once more. Snow falls on Daffodils. Morning-glory climbs icicles. On one calendar it's Persidian August. Meteors plunge.

When the cave-children are halfway down a slope, that's the time the fire goes out.

On the distant edge of a distant beach are ten mirrors. Inside that first circle there are seven mirrors. Inside that circle there are three.

A battered sign reads, "End of Project."

Past that sign is where the world ends & is a crescent of beach & beyond the beyond of that, there's darkness. Beyond that black veil, there's a crescent of stars. Beyond that? More blackness.

Caught by the curve of land behind the beach is the Mockingbird Motel. The motel has a circular courtyard, and in that circle is a square house.

- This is like brackets - think the children.

- First, there is a crescent of land, as thin as a scythe, and following the line of the scythe, there is curved ocean. Then the blank -

"You've learned well" whisper the whisperers.

And then another whisper: *End of project.*

Well, almost.

I breathe.

I dip my quill into red ink, lean over the magnifying glass, move the red chair closer to the table.

Sidewalks fill with heat & light & then melt – and still I write.

Still.

<u>Gabriel</u>:

In the heat he asks "Where am I?
In the sunlight he asks again: seeking
answers from the heart of this shimmer of heat.
"Is there someone that I am supposed to meet?"

Heat soaks Gabriel's robe. His red hair fizzes and curls. Reaching inside the back-pack he finds and hefts a small metal pot to check for dents, reflecting a distorted image of himself, hair fuzzy as a peach, white streaking through his hair like opium threaded through hard hashish. He's suddenly become old & what was once powerful & bold in his eyes has reduced in light and force.

How did that happen?

When did that happen?

Gabriel is no longer busy, but, of course, must look busy – as if he knows what's going on. Forgetfulness has scrubbed his hopes, his childhood, the songs he used to sing in late night bars. He is alone with thought. The longer he stares at his reflection in his dipper (his trusty dipper) the more things change. In an hour, he sees his beard turn totally white, crow's feet now time-lapse his eye-crinkles, eyelids turn into puffy clouds flowing across the field on the mountain.

How does that happen?

When does that happen?

Before he stood on this plain he was young! His face had few wrinkles, there were only faint traces of white in his red beard & his joints didn't creak like they do now. Also he was wearing blue jeans & a black T-shirt. And he had no gut.

Reaching down, he grasps flab. When his gut sags, he speaks.

"What the hell's happened?

Where's my prick gone?

Nesting inside of me now – that's where, gone wherever time has gone. What are they feeding me? I remember a story from childhood all about Rip Van Winkle but I have no memory of lying down and sleeping.

One minute I was trying to find my way back to my house, past a new car parked in the driveway, and then there was a flash of light of some kind & it made my eyes water. Eyes watering so much that I couldn't see who approached me.

I swore that I knew my house & the flowers I had planted & the small fence that I had built with my own hands, built with the neighbor.

Another flash of light.

My neighbor?

We took the line dusted with lime & flicked it, each of us holding one end. It left a clear straight mark on every picket & we used an electric saw to lop off the tops of the pickets.

Why is it that people think they have no impact –? - for there he is in my memory. He's an unexpected beacon & once upon a time he knew my grandfather. Sometimes I remember – and it was, at the time, a nothing-special moment. Rare. That's what I remember; the nothing-special things - those what? I remember what?"

-::- Flash -::-

"That was the time before time held me in its maw & taught me a new law of wrinkles – how lines form anew each hour & weave a spider's web of flesh, a net to hold my face in place. After the white flash, I held on to the fence to keep from falling & it felt real & clean and true. There were voices in the white flash, then darkness & then greater darkness & then I was outside, looking at a mountain from this field.

Then. Then. Then!

I have a sudden memory of dashing away. I can clearly recall the running shoes that I'd bought that day. They were *AirSports* & were brand new & white & every bit as clean as I kept the picket fence.

I look down at my shoes and they're the same ones that took me through the field – scuffs and marks from hiking but still brand new. So, obviously, little time has passed since the flash – just enough to put me on this mountain where my traveling companions have left me."

-::- Flash -::-

Speech ended, he curls up, inside his robe upon the rocks.

Gabriel does not dream & does not move. Only the sun moves as it slides across the day & over his face and into the woods, a wheel turning in a grave.

Clouds dim the sun. Cool winds replace heat.

He distinctly hears a low growl pulling him from his sleep into late afternoon.

It's followed by a snorting snuffling sound & the clicking crack of twigs crashing. The quick sharp cry of a small animal is followed by total stillness.

In his mind is Italian.

"Do I know Italian? "

Ma poi ch'i' fui al piè d'un colle giunto...

"Where is that coming from?"

là dove terminava quella valle...

"...Where?"

che m'avea di paura il cor compunto...

"Pretend I will, I can't hear at all

Pretend I can't hear...

...It."

Moloch:

Wrapped in sleep,
bound to another:
unborn Siamese twins

folded one into the other.

- dreaming -

"His dreams seem like mine because he kicks and yells while falling. I am told that, in sleep, I kick and yell and grind my teeth and sometimes drool. I can't recall (even with the aid of exquisite drugs) what I dream or even if I dream. Everything goes dark & my heart slows & a great dark mouth eats me.

That is how I fall asleep – buckled over lower teeth, crushed, against upper teeth. But I wouldn't call those dreams. That's just life.

I hear others coming. The shift is changing so I must return to where he keeps me. The good doc still sleeps tho' his kicking stops when I try and make him weep. His breathing is shifting to be more like mine. Calm, steady – waiting, until that day when I suck marrow from his spine.

Crack.
Snap.
Slurp.

Moloch moves slowly.
Crisp as old leaves spiral in the fall.

Pages fall to the floor and the doctor wakes up.
     Something about leaves, and…fall? Starched in new whites, he doesn't look at his clipboard. Instead, eyes averted, he lifts the new sheets, shaking them as if the writing could slide black dots down the page and onto the floor where, when the daily cleaning is done, no trace of them would remain.

Perhaps there might remain a few silent dots of dirt.

The good Doc folds & rips and tears the sprawled writing until it falls in torn snowflakes across the floor.

Snow drifts along an empty hall.

He doesn't bother to pick up the flakes.

The trail of paper snow crosses the room & drifts along the hall.

Nel mezzo del cammin di nostra vita
Mi ritovai per una selva oscura
Ché la devitta via era smarrita

Gabriel stands up hastily re-slinging his backpack. Darkness rolls a bouncing ball towards his nine-pin-life as he runs into a section of the forest where there are no screams. Tree fingers tug at his backpack while he pushes towards deeper forest, putting as much space between him & whatever creatures are causing small animals to yelp and whimper.

Trees squeak. Gabriel pushes his hand against an ancient oak. Something pushes back. A high-pitched vibration; a thin keening begins & he cannot tell if this sound comes from his ears or the forest.

Missing, even from himself & his name forgotten, with no memories of the woods that earlier looked like a lame furry caterpillar wrapped in a warm green towel. Leaning against the tree & weeping. Its rough face comforts him, the pattern of the bark pressing dentingly against his face.

His beard is tangling with old dried moss that traces the edge of the tree. Bowing his head, Gabriel prays that grace will descend from the dark sky to cover his tight shoulders.

-::- Flash -::-

Light glows from tangled roots. Phosphorescent sheen splashes old growth trees, light grows, glinting across wings of hovering bees, turning Gabriel's running shoes the color of churned butter. Falling to his knees, he asks the tree, aloud, for precious shelter.

Opening his eyes again he peers into the tangle of roots where a cave is lit by growing crystals that cluster; small, delicate, rainbow-spilling, sharding. He hears a snuffling animal's coughing just behind his arched back. Without delay he plunges through the roots of the tree.

The cave is deeper than he thought at first. Feet zooming & scraping past the roots, Gabriel's butt catches up with him and slides along the earth. His shoulders bounce off a rock.

Hair plucked by twigs his face is scratched before he slides clear of the earth.

Falling down there's no ground beneath his feet.

-::- Flash -::-

Falling.

Falling

-::- Flash -::-

Eve:

What Eve does write
when she holds pages in her heart:
how she prays for her talent
to be kicked into a jump-start.

A t one time Eve was always on the edge of being happy. Excited, she peeped over back lots or gazed into the snow drift flare & glare of a screen where she stared at people born in altered pages of her scripts.

That was at her own 'once upon a time.' She watched Cinema's flickering loop as it forever paraded head-to-end on screen. Now, all energy's left the screen in a bone-head sacrifice to executive beliefs of what might move a paying audience to cough up dough. Pale sticks of flat-face actors began to speak words that she never wrote; they moved through bleached versions of fake grief. Eve wondered where the real people had gone. It was for certain that they no longer existed in movies, in theatres, in television, or in song. It's not enough to make someone a billionaire. It's not enough to have someone fall down an elevator and climb back out to shoot a few dozen people. Should be some real people. Not screen tough. Weak. No perfect teeth glinting at the world. Just a couple of real people.

Where have they all gone?

Where is the fat man in a Garth-Brooks-look-alike Black & Blue suit who last fall lay upon the grass watching a group of kids play baseball?

He came to mind, Eve's then-working mind, because it was better to day-dream, than to see what had been done to her cherished dream-scripts. Once upon that fading time, she'd loitered in the park with a favorite book & carried a loaf of bread, some good cheese, a concealed jug of wine & her 'just-in-case' Mace. She'd gone as a then-diligent writer, to spy on people. Eavesdrop on random folks.

It was that time of year when there should be falling leaves. But, in Los Angeles only heat fell from blurred trees.

"The deciduous nature of light..." she thought but didn't write it down - believing she'd remember it.

A mistake.

Of a sudden, a baseball game; a vision for Eve of everyday life. Kids with crooked teeth, the name of *Steed's Storage Units* stenciled upon their mesh and polyester shirts.

So real it hurt her all-paid-for & perfect teeth.

One man's bicuspids were slippery yellow; he was overweight, his gut sagged over his silver buckle. When he smiled, smoke leaked through gaps between his teeth and, when he shouted, more smoke blew out. Drifted over his star-buttoned jacket.

"Hit it, Shadow Boy" he screamed.

It was a poem delivered as a joke to all the kids, who looked and laughed & didn't change their pace a jot, for this was a Dad, who was widely known to mouth off a lot. Eve remained transfixed, this man had spoken in a way that she knew could give new life to all her scripts. New life to all she wrote. Tears spilled from her eyes. This was for her a miracle.

Her eyes refilled and two new chill drops sped down her cheeks. And then she remembered who she was and what she did & taking out her leather bound pad of beige paper wrote it down, couldn't figure why speech lost energy as her pen moved & decided she could always revise it later. She forgot what she'd written down and why "Hit it shadow boy" had lost its power.

She did take a moment to write, "Once you start crying, you can't stop."

Clouds blowing across a brown sky tattered her memory into clouds; the wind tore off chunks of memory the way a starving woman might rip apart cheap French bread. Before Eve finished her own expensive wine and crusty bread, she'd forgotten the man in his jacket – the cries from teammates, and she left behind (on a picnic bench) her leather bound notebook and pen.

Later that night, back in current time – having lived through winter and, of course, the fall into the spring; as memory faded and leaves unfurled; before she fell asleep in what she knew only as "now" she saw the face of that man in the black & blue jacket. Over his head, a giant baseball whirled atop the center of a shadow.

She thought it was a puzzling image but looking for her notebook to write it down, couldn't find it & wondered if she'd ever owned a notebook or just dreamed it was in the world & not her mind. She blinked and closed her eyes. Before she fell asleep she prayed "What is happening? What is happening to me? Please answer. If you care, tell me. Tell me, please! Come near."

No answer in that springtime night.

Eve wakes in pulsing fright; scared because her memory has rattled out a pinball thought – she must go to a meeting. Greeting herself in the mirror, she chants:

"Oh yes, I'm supposed to go…." and she hesitates. "...to... oh yes... a meeting. I must prepare – use all my ..."

She falters & takes a shower that lasts an hour. Later (where does time go?) it is another time and she's still damp & wrinkled from her marathon shower

"Is this another shower?
 Is it the same?
I mix and match.
My brain has spilled time.
No crime."

Eve is supposed to be on her way to a meeting at *Starbucks* in Santa Monica. She'd written, at some time or other, the time, date & place on a wall calendar. She also placed it inside her missing daybook, on scraps of paper beside the stove (where she's left burning on low a rear burner while the oven's warming.)

The same message, unnoticed, is scrawled across a chalkboard, where she used to keep notes on plot structure or amusing lines that'd come to her in sleep & later made her smile and wonder "Who wrote that? What fine style."

There is, on this chalkboard, the huge reminder "Starbucks on Monday" – but the only link her mind can make with 'meeting' and with 'Starbucks' is not of meetings, nor of pitch, nor scripts – but with Seattle.

She tries her best to remember what she'd meant by writing "Starbucks" such a strange name and a date and time on notes and chalkboards, & on the calendar and in her bent and battered daybook.

Eve remembers three things:
The first?
She still has a pen.
The second thing she remembers is that for nights, in her sleep, she's flown over her back yard up past the circling

helicopters of the Hollywood skies & zoomed through brown clouds towards the blue moon sailing down, down, down across the mist that lies upon the ocean. She recalls that planes still fly along the coast from LA towards the cooler ocean of the Pacific Northwest where fog can roll and hold you underneath the past.

And then her *third* memory – credit cards!

Staring into the mirror, she tries an affirmation:

"I can fly. I can use my magic plastic card and fly. Fly towards the cooler ocean; can walk on streets that are cool and wet. Before I forget what it is that I yet am meant to do – before the day when life may move through my memory and erase, without a trace, besides a noctilucent flux, like an eraser smears a much-used day-glo whiteboard, these thoughts: I will call a taxi & have it bear me like a chariot to the airport. And with my plastic magic I shall wrap around me an airplane of silver fabric and it will, through metallic air, take me and my plans to Seattle. I will step from the plane and let cool damp breezes fly me to the ocean."

She pauses, dazed by what she's said, and stares back at herself from the mirror.

"Now, that's one hell of an affirmation."

Miracles abound for Eve as she prepares to leave Tinsel Town – her adopted city. Not the least is that she remembers the number for the taxi & in miraculous follow-up, the taxi arrives at the exact time when the dispatcher said it would.

"...I'm on my way to a meeting – a meeting with the Pacific Ocean, it's set up in Seattle, I read it written large all over the inside of my house" she says as she forgets to lock her doors or punch in the code to her *Armed Response* alarm system but "What the Heck" she says to the Cabby, "It's only a foolish old house."

She does remember to take 'mad money' and cram it in her purse. She has easy traffic on the way to the airport. And when she asks the driver, in her rambling disconnected way, if he knows a man in a midnight blue shirt & jacket who likes to cheer for children in a baseball game, the driver – instead of asking her name & driving her to a hospital does something much better. Instead of enjoying *less* he turns out to be a man who's fond of *more*.

He's a kind man who comes from a small town south of the border where, when someone loses their mind, no one calls them crazy. A small town where, when someone misplaces their mind, why no one takes them to a hospital. So called crazies are allowed to roam the universe of a small town, doing what they want, until, in time, they find their mind, usually in the same place where they'd lost it.

So the driver simply remarks, "Perhaps, some day, I will meet this man. Perhaps, I will get a call to pick him up in a park where children are playing baseball & because of the kindness of your words, I now know what he looks like – the man in the midnight blue jacket who likes to cheer at his children's games. I will drive him to Seattle so he may be with you."

And then they are at the airport & her thoughts remain with her close enough to take her to the counter, get her a ticket, take her through the closed-in ramp, have her buckle her seatbelt; longing for the damp and salt of her Starbucks meeting with the ocean. She no longer thinks – she feels.

Eve sits through the coffee and buys no snacks, gets off the plane, into another taxi which takes her to her meeting with the sea.

"I remembered my meeting," is her first triumphant thought. "I have not forgotten it."

She removes her clothing as if she were running on Mulholland again but this time held by the true desire that salty water always needs its fire. Setting her clothes and ID on a trash bin she lights them as if the fire were the torch of Leif the Lucky's funeral.

The Vinland curl smudges night-time skies. She burns her past & the smoke rolls around her.

Eve wonders what makes flames grow higher and higher, makes smoke clouds twist and turn in Viking shadow shapes that build, in Seattle skies, the form of her dream town, the picket fences reflecting light on this night preceding the night of the dark moon.

Around her neck she hangs her purse: intense purple, a night color suspended by a golden cord with noontime-glitter threaded through it. Clouds hold smoke. Clouds hold the faces of the newborn.

All ID burned, she jams her purse with mad money, swings the purse round and round her naked neck and plunges back into the ocean's arms, hearing the sound of the Pacific voice singing away in her inner ear.

Diving through breath-bubbles, she finds a perfect shell & holding it, she rises to snag a floating log with its limbs spread wide apart like holy arms playing an accordion. And in those arms she sets the shell & in the mouth of the shell she places the purse, saying, "This is a fine offering."

She pushes the log with the tide, watches it dip in a small breeze. The tide and ocean both accept her offering of the purse & she swims towards Seattle's shoreline.

Then she runs along the beach praying for a time-wind. Only thing to appear are two cops & a beating red light.

"Hey, in Seattle people pay attention when your tits hang out," is her only comment to the cops & the night.

When read her rights, all she can find to say is, "Naked I have fallen to earth after seeing the sights."

The Cops wrap her like a taco, folding her warm into a blanket & ask if there is anything more they might do before they leave the shore and take her to a welcoming hospital.

She replies, and her breasts (that had charmed all, from Props men to Studio Heads) peep over the red blanket. "Why, certainly. If you have a moment, I would like an apple & after that apple has been eaten & I am directed to my tree, I would like to find my Adam."

She remains quiet until the hospital where they ask her name & she replies softly.

"Eve. My name is Eve and I require some sky, an ocean, perhaps a bonfire. And, oh yes, I do require an imperfect garden."

The Making of the land:

While all the children watch, the storyteller splits into two Beings.

The Left is Maud, the Right is Ern. His hooves have melted into feet; her eyes have melted into blue pools that bubble, and from them light in blue sheets plays along the crescent sand.

And each recalls a name.

There is Eve and Luna di Luna. There is Thomas of the Piano, and Stephen of the wards. There is Yemaya of the Ocean & Arrow of the Skies. Queen Mab sees, amongst the few trees, that lights are fluttering. There's a video buzz of hummingbirds & she recalls that she is Mab of the Faeries. In the darkness there's the Man in the Midnight Blue Jacket and he begins to awaken. His buttons are stars. He looks at the wall as if he's watching a baseball game. That's enough for him.

And as soon as all know that there are names, well, of a sudden, there are hands and although they know there is no head above the shoulders they see themselves in each other's faces. Yet, they do not think for this is too early for thought. Too late for thinking.

And there is land to be made. So far, there nothing but a circle, a square and a crescent beach, and above all is hungry darkness rimmed with gold-star teeth. Such sparklers have eaten almost all the world, now they wait. Seven children between the last bite & starting all over again. Glitter teeth closing.

All we know from the stories, from the smoke from the fire, from losing our heads all over the world is that we already know what to do. No matter what, we always know what to do. And my hand trembles as the scarlet letters move under the microscope, as the table shakes, darkness moving across the floor toward the legs.

Write slowly, hand moving exactly – like children's hands.

I'm reaching for the last two points of the world.

At the tipping points of the curved beach are Eastern Island Beings. Each stands and raises their hands, their fingers of coal reaching upwards, and from the darkness their finger magnets draw from the endless black deep earth, and it slides hissing from the sky towards them.

They raise hands even higher, finger spreading like atolls – the black sky, that comforting blanket of earth, living, spinning, the deep beautiful ebony of endless darkness. Shadowing beautiful night swings towards the beach, towards the seven children, the Beings who always (with Tiki patience) awaiting endless soil.

O...

...see what's drawn from the night, towards the sky-born buttons of a midnight blue jacket. Earth pulls earth towards them.

The children stand next to pumiced smiles. Reaching out, as if holding a dark deep blanket, they grip the edges of a vast blanket of loam, and pull it towards them & the more they pull, the more it stretches. The more it stretches, the more they grow. And the more they grow, the more increases their strength, and as they pull, they tilt & the earth rolls towards midnight & turns into marbles.

As they snap the blanket and shake it, Easter Island Beings tremble & crack apart along their seams & tower until they double & triple & quadruple.

New earth falls on their heads & they bend & break & float in melting fire-rimmed earth, and they glow, and the planet's on fire, everywhere except the island.

O...

... broken pieces of the Eater Island Beings, split again & again & again. Splitting, bubbling with insect delight.

Fire is now boiling & once again the giant heads split & crack & disintegrate.

"This is why we came here", they think

It is midnight of the first night.

We are no longer scared of the dark.

Not even one of us.

The Music Girl:

Seeking her true name,
the Music Girl searches forest;
swims past aspen groves, dives
into the center of each brook.

When she finds no trace of what her new name might be, Music Girl leaves Nature's realm of gut-hunch feeling where her name might be found. She does not wait for an outside omen to reveal her name; weaving it in sleep into the flowers laced beneath her rumbled pillow. Instead, a reading willow, she drapes and dips above a stream of books – ripples of other people's waking reveries.

Late night, lit by flashlight's golden coil, she reads till morning while turning pages to fight her way with Beowulf, standing right beside him on underwater soil when he battles Grendel's mother. Before she closes the book, she wishes she could help Grendel's mother.

"Who was she? That mother; the mom of Grendel? Just someone different, that's all. Someone who lived in caves like we used to, like we will again. Cities smoking, us in front of a thin fire. Caves? Someone who lived in caves? No need to kill that scaled & sacred mother!"

Her heart is not with Beowulf.

Her heart, tho' her mind be crooked, is not within miles of the weary warriors of the world. "O, so sad, all these baby warriors.

Golem? Someone I knew? All dead. Resting. Their hurting heads – their death in places – well, dead is dead, all gone."

She fights the Iliad as her pages turn; sails the Odyssey into the night with her book-light, cheers for the Sirens as she puts in a battered bookmark, speaks a new language with the Bröntes; follows Dante where few poets dare to go and dog-ears every third page, finds her own chilled circle, thaws it with the heat of Donne, flies into the sun with Icarus, zooms back and forth through time and space, one moment gazing on Helen's face, the next deciding to be, forever, Holden Caulfield's mate. With all this reading she still cannot find the name that will click in her mind; no name to become her own.

When she has dragged all the books to her home she slides through Netted-E-Book-Libraries & into recent time. And still she cannot find her name. Until this very night. Her parents buy wine to go with their fried chicken. Washing down greasy skin with chilled wine; licking their fingers while changing channels. Greasy lips, blue from reflected television.

The Music Girl sees on the family TV-trays a bottle also pouring blue light into the night. Drawn to it, moth-like, she makes her way past the cluttered table towards the TV trays, picks up the bottle, angles it towards the screen and reads the label, as a song hums vibrating her neck.

"Why," she says, "finding my true name is, O, so simple. I didn't really need to seek, it would have come to me so much sooner if I'd only looked close to home." She speaks aloud the wine bottle's label.

"This is my name – *Luna di Luna*! 'Luna,' for short."

Knowing truth, , she sets back the bottle, walks past her never-startled parents to her room, packs with great care a few belongings, travels with a name so new that she carries it like elfin baggage.

"I" she sings to the waning moon "am Luna di Luna, your earth-tumbled sister, ready to share with whatever world will have me, what you have taught me, Grandmother Moon."

She has only one more book to read. It appears in the corner of her bedroom when a time-wind blows backwards. The title catches her eye: *This Is What I Must Remember*. And so it is. The last book in the library is also the first. All night she reads & when she dozes at dawn & she awakens to the noon-time news & the first delivery of KFC. When she woke up, it was to discover that another time-wind had blown the book ahead to the cave.

The next evening at Burlington she boards the Greyhound for the West.

"I will not stop until I see Pacific waters where I may dip my feet. I bring a faded book or two, some changes of clothing & my greatest gifts, my hands, my heart, my wide-open eyes."

The bus pulls out of the station, she closes her eyes, splaying her fingers across the keys of an invisible keyboard. Luna leans & nods above the unseen black and white making it ripple in the night. She vibrates with a Glen Gould humming and sets an old Blues player strumming along with an energy he has not felt since he'd, in his younger days, accompanied Ralph the swimming pig, at the Colorado river's bend where archaeologists said the oldest sign of women and men in North America began. But that's beside the point 'cause what he feels now he hasn't felt since as a ten-year-old he played in his first sawdust floor beer-joints.

He takes from the overhead rack the twelve string that he's bringing back home to play for one last time. He has the ashes of Mary, his dancing old-time sweetie. He's wearing a very well-worn red & yellow shirt with blue-fringes. "Blue for the blues," he smiles. His urn is painted with snowflakes falling on Los Angeles. Stars pin eyes to the city's shadowed face. The urn shakes as he plays. Strumming with what he hears beneath the girl's humming sound, he grounds his guitar in the song being born. He plays along with the very center of her name, while Luna sings the strings.

"Oh" she asks "how can you do that? Play the tune that's playing in my head?"

"I watch your fingers, sweetie, and if the middle of the seat in front of you may be taken as middle C, why I can tell through these tired old eyes of mine what tune to play with those who take a journey so they may play for those who live next to a distant sea. Besides," he adds "you are humming and I can easy match that with my strumming."

He leans in to play & her humming turns into her song & her throat opens & her music grows.

"I'm Luna," she cries & sings this name into the woven edges of her song.

"Pleased to meet you, my name is Lefty" he crinkles, "& happy to be able to play along. Lefty & Luna. Nice." His smile widens & over his face there spreads a fresh network of wrinkles.

Luna notices the urn. It glows as the lights go off.

"Who's that?"

"Love of my life. ashes of my ashes. Feet dancing in the dust."

Luna begins to sing, a sweet song for Mary. Sprites from the Vermont forest blink & sparkle at the windows of the bus. Lefty gets the tune, and he plays along. Even the wheels on the bus go round & round the tune. Tires hiss, lights sparkle. The urn snows on itself.

The bus sails across the night. Twin beams suck sparks from the eyes of tiny deer, paused as if on top of a wedding cake.

"Shoot," observes the driver, "This is why I drive this magic bus. And it's not just for the job, the money to raise a big-screen-3d-plus-whatever-they-happen-to-come-up-with so-called Entertainment center television for my sweetie. It's because, on my bus, all of us are on a great adventure & when our trip is through, if I do my driving as I should, you will all know exactly what it is that you climbed on this big blue bus to do. And it ain't for the money."

"But the bus isn't blue, honey" shouts back a rhyming passenger & the driver smiles, about to do what he has waited many years to do. He pulls over by the forest edge & taking out a dozen spray cans, passes them around.

Passengers rush out to spray and laugh, in rhythm, to the music that still flows from the bus.

"Does this mean I can smoke in the bathroom?" asks a man in red suspenders. And the driver smiles, "Means only that you may spray-paint the hell out of this bus!"

And pretty soon the bus is, indeed, Big Blue. And it skids back into the highway, making its way straight through the highway of the mind, direct to you. The driver sings his thoughts over the PA system. His eyes glisten with Big Blue excitement, lit by new thoughts, mixed with the songs of Luna & Lefty.

The bus wings through the night, outlined blue against the moon. Passengers snapping cobalt fingers now hum, & do lean against the chilled-down windows. If they aren't singing, they accompany the song with rhythmic beating hearts. They exhale against a window, watching mist expand and contract in music. Some lovers sing along to the rhythm with their kisses. Somehow, deep inside, they know each journey is special – but this one?

Oh my. They know they are driving in a big old blue song that will allow all to sing along, to be part of a journey in a magic bus outlined against the sky, that they travel in a tune, a tune that drives the bus.

Way later, they stop at Swift Current, and Luna notices a revival meeting. Something smells very good, and tho' she has little money, she wanders over to the park. There's a bar-b-q set up, and women in odd garments, and at least twenty men who look like ZZ Top.

"I'm really on the road," she thinks. And she eats a hot dog, given to her by one of the ZZ clones. She starts singing, and all the other look-alikes gather around her, and with Luna di Luna in the middle, they sing, oddly enough, "*Knee Deep in the Big Muddy*" and suddenly, all people in the park join in. She calls out words, and the ZZ folk all sing back. Big Blue beeps, and she heads back to the bus. The voices float with her, and the town itself keeps singing:

When Luna settles by the window, her reflection shivers over the park, where ZZ & friends all sing, and now the guitars belt into the song – and the bus is silent; the words ripple down the aisle.

Singing what everyone's saying.

Luna's new song begins to form.

And when she sleeps it finds her & slips into her dream, seamlessly.

Deep in the lee of her mind, it roils, rolls, and tickles her fingers. She dreams of a piano – a green piano.

Seattle

By now the moon has swung through quarters
shrunk to dark moon down from full
dipped its way thru time lapse clouds
Rolled thru new light to Seattle.

All our roads lead to Seattle; by car, by plane, through security gates of airports, bus terminals, in ambulance & emergency helicopter. Our friends have risen and dipped, sped & braked, rushed & slowed, dreaming & awake, conscious & unconscious.

Strapped to gurneys; arms linked to police, walking in from the ocean, singing & crying, leaping & almost dying they've all made their way to this curved city by the sea – have smelled the forest rotting in the distance & heard the cries of eagles near cloud-covered mountains; witnessed the look of other eagles linked claw-to-claw/whirly-gigging from the sky into the harbor.

Here are horns, steamer blasts, jets whining; calliopes from amusement parks, lights of Ferris wheels against the night sky, gulls angled into the morning sky. Fresh crab, grilled fish, pretzels, lame bands rehearsing in crooked garages, hoping, hoping for hope from those who give no hope; dressing up for Saturday night; dressing down for Friday night; going out retro-bowling on weekday nights. Endless construction in the exact lane you need. Horns, cheers, waves on the shore, with the ebb and flow of traffic. People sleeping in alleyways, people sleeping in the woods, people watching their windows being cleaned while they sip lattes and admire the view, coffee, more coffee & brown bags for half-filled bottles.

Yeah.

Seattle.

Her voice continues to sing in the ears of our mastless gang, hooking the inner ear, tugging on their foreheads, spinning their charkas, dancing their dreams, lifting, for a moment, the veil.

The secret is to untie oneself from the mast.

Quickly.

Before the knots set.

Seattle becomes the center of the web of some very crazy spiders.

One filigreed tendril of the web hooks on a large tree in Vermont, catching dew drops & fairy lights, glittering as it sags over an empty fountain, threads and rests on a clock tower, tugs against the window of a second-hand bookstore in Montpelier, until book dust shakes loose & floating through the glass, does dust the web. A puzzled bear looks down from the hills and when she sleeps, shares the dream with her cubs.

The web joins the tops of aspen trees; flash of maple, buzzing of power lines, hum of transformers. It waffle-prints bumpers of cars & drapes empty highways where billboards aren't allowed to live. It crosses the fields of Plainsfield, wrinkling like laundry on a line over the grounds of Goddard College – resting on the old stone stairs of an upper garden & crossing the country to hum and click in the clock-house morning.

In Cascade Locks this web drapes over Arrow's father.

Nights & nights and mornings & mornings have passed and he's learned what departed with Arrow. Lonely, he's looked in the mirror & yelled at himself as there is no-close-to-falling-hand Arrow to hit anymore, nor to shake. In the morning there's no half-assed breakfast assembled by a sleepy boy; no fried-to-dried-ratshit bacon, no burned toast & no runny eggs. There's no congealed ketchup on the table, no crystallizing pool of maple syrup, no still-damp socks from the faulty dryer. Arrow has gone.

His son who never carried ID; his son who always said he'd run away, his son who almost had the cops call about his vanishing – skateboard and all, from Cascade Locks. His hand was on the phone, he'd almost punched the necessary buttons – *almost* but not quite.

This father roams the town, a bottle in his hand. He sleeps, as on this morning, in alleyways & in his sleep tries to brush away the web – his hand sticking to web and shoulder.

He shrugs and sleeps some more.

Blood crusts on his lip, his nose drips. His blanket of newspapers has blown away & the web is tugging at his heart. He dreams of a glowing spider in the sky, its golden thread catching & splitting light. He dreams a rainbow that holds the day & tacks it together with the night. When the dad turns, the web shakes and trembles & dewdrops burn their last like stretched glass comets falling. When he snores the net pulls in & then the net shakes out. He snores again.

The web trembles along the alleyway, along the highway, high enough to scrap the leaves off the top of tractor trailers, & the leaves fall & curl & form a leaf storm & headlights are put on although the day is only grey. One thread vibrates & pulls taut – sunlight breaking from the arms of an old cloud & like corn syrup dripping in a mouth does gild the web that hooks to Mab's abandoned house.

A window has been left open, a hatch uplifted has not been returned & bolted & the threads make their way into the house, pulling like a full clothesline in a hurricane. Turning, webbing over half-open books in the library, dog-eared books in the bathroom, new books in the living room, old books in the guest room, & unpacked books stacked, stacked, stacked in the hallway by the front door. It gathers dust as it webs diplomas, awards, photos of forgotten colleges, pictures of tenure-parties, a garter from a wedding, a framed copy of divorce papers, the pictures of dead parents, the pictures of dead grandparents, a photo of a special day, the drawings from her child who grew up, left home & forgot to write, forgot to call – all webbing together.

When was the beginning of the great forgetting?

Where am I -?- was in her first set of questions -?- who am I -?- the set of last questions.

The name of Beowulf is scratched into a wall. The liquor cabinet has doors that never close. There are containers of take-out food, there are home-delivery boxes. There are collector's CDs, there are even-older albums next to a collection of post cards. Abandoned stamp collections lie near a magnifying glass.

The house still breathes. Dust circles windows. Thousands of small spiders hatch inside light fixtures. Crazy-happy to be alive. Rappelling into the empty house, filling the rooms. Grey & brown & furry, vibrating, running, gathering shooting fire needles out their butts.

The house shimmers & nervous neighbors wonder what the hell is happening.

That spider web. The big one. That time. The big one. All webs joining, all over this spinning planet. That web.

One guy, a neighbor looks at it and feels there's something he's meant to remember – he holds a tabby cat in his arms. The cat's ears are fluffed with fur & she watches a spider drop before her. She doesn't bat it with her paw, instead she climbs a trellis & sits upon the roof, adjusting haunches on the buckled shake roof. She looks to the sky, directly into the sun. This, her old buckled body says, may be the web I've been awaiting.

Satisfied, she stretches languid on the roof, her rippled back soaking up the morning sunshine, fur growing warm. A spider lands upon her back. She doesn't care. She lets the sun warm up her ears. She looks around – other cats are on other rooftops. All settle in, for they know this could take a while. They wait and lick their paws while time-winds rustle their whiskers.

One finds a Time-wind hidden near a mouse hole he's been watching, he reaches in to catch it and is whirled to Christopher Smart's roof top. Home again!

One finds another time-wind under a loose shingle. She releases it, and finds herself stretching as the world begins. "Cats first!" she observes. "They got it right!"

The rest of the critters wait. They look at the moon & taste the air.

One filament of the spider's web forms angles from a nearby palm tree far away in Los Angeles, to drape over Beverly Hills – the web is pulsing but only a few people look up to see the sky & so it isn't noticed. An early morning tourist with a camera sees a cable in his viewfinder & plucks on the thread stuck to his camera. It sounds like a damp mandolin string. Morning makes the net hum.

A man in a midnight blue jacket wakes up in a cheap motel & sees that threads have crossed his window in the shape of a baseball diamond. He reaches under his bed and pulls out a glove; a ball. In the sunlight, brown-yellow in Los Angeles, he watches the baseball as he tosses it towards the ceiling, catches it as it falls & throws it up again. He sings, and catches. Someone thumps on the wall from the next room. He sings louder and the ball hits the ceiling. Thumps begin from the room above. He throws and smiles & then he sings some more.

The web travels along the street, trembles through the valley, finds a wrought-iron gate, climbs & sticks & inside Eve's 'all-alone-am-I' house, drapes over the trophies, photos of stars from the forties, & animal actors of the fifties. There's a snap of Eve as a little girl at a "Hollywood Birthday Party" – with Stan Laurel & her best friend Timmy. Another shot of her kissing Timmy & then of Timmy waving goodbye.

The web sticks together memos, post-it notes & signs pasted to a dusty computer & a jammed dot-matrix printer. The signs say "I must remember…" In lipstick on a mirror is written, "I must remember."

The web goes back in time to George's Cove and joins Melody Lo, and Ariel, hooks to the telescope aimed towards the sky, floats above an outlined 'widow's walk' & trembles from the eyepiece of a telescope towards the moon & through a singing voice, to find a ship of ice, and finds its Skipper wheeling hard-a-port. It shifts the rudder & travels galaxies, threads through black vortexes that stretch and double web lines back to earth and below.

The web finds a cave and travels through the cave, over the smoking fire, out the smoke vent, down the slope & once there attaches to Easter Island heads, to seven-year old foreheads, and glows, and enters crescent water & attaches to the forehead of a sleeping giant woman. And all time stops, as if listening to the distant sound of bagpipes, wondering where that sound originates. Perhaps the moon?

And then - the web goes out the window & it catches sunshine. It is bathed in fog; it reflects bumper-to-bumper, it crosses fields where arrowheads are buried; it's in streams; it is on dry lands.

Spiders all over the country run & tend & mend & feel: feel what is happening & they tremble & hair rises on their legs & the Katydids hear them & they sing together & the web hums & there's a sound all through Seattle & the sound stops even the early morning-skip-school-and-keep-playing set & all traffic stops again & there is a *something* – something without words that makes the whole city stop and listen.

– Listen. Listen. Listen –

I'm still in the cave.

I'm all the way down the slope.

Yet I'm already half-way up the slope.

I'm in the waterfall. I am the waterfall.

Still I'm in Seattle.

I'm in Vermont.

Still I'm in Los Angeles

I've left Newfoundland.

I'm sailing in a ship of ice over Mumbai, tacking to turn towards Iceland. Sea anchoring next to Istanbul, shadows, grey, white night, flaring, we look at a crescent moon.

My ship of ice has melted and I am falling thru the sky.

I hit land.

I arise from granite. Carved gargoyle now, I climb to the top of a cathedral and write in memories. Centuries pass, and the building crumbles. I fall again.

I crash through Newfoundland. I sail with pirates.

I sing with Susie Hopkins.

Still.

All at once – everywhere – everyone.
And at the center a red chair. I dip my quill into scarlet
ink. I write…
…in the middle of a meadow…
…beside an old wooden table…
…I whisper to a patient.
I sleep. Chart falling slo-mo to the floor.
I would reach for the electric switch, but I am dreaming.

Almost.

The Making of the Air:

Once land has expanded throughout the globe, the children brush cobwebs from their foreheads & then walk towards the sea, but the earth holds them. When they take a step, the step steps towards them, a *something* presses them as they near where the air stops; a curved nothing, that they feel rising at the same angle as they approach.

Steps.

Arrow takes a dark rock and throws it, but it stops, held by the something that quivers. He walks beneath it, looks up to see the pitted porous blackness, held solidly in place.

Eve digs and finds nothing. Her side hurts with the digging. Each of the children, from young Thomas to little Luna, now hears a whisper in their left ear – "…the future is behind you."

Every child hears a whisper in their right ear. "The past is in front of you..."

And with a sound high above them, whispers join to chant..."The future comes through you, and stops now."

Arrow squints and looks ahead, under the shadow of the rock, and, as he looks ahead to the past, he hears the sounds of wheels on asphalt. He doesn't know yet what that hiss is. But it draws him and, as he moves, he sees beyond the sound a small boy at a fort & there's an arrow in his shoulder & further ahead into the distant past, another seven-year-old boy – brown skinned, is running up a ladder. The sun is so strong, that he opens his arms to hold it, and before that small boy, way ahead, at a new horizon in the forward distance, as far ahead as he can see, there is a blue & yellow baby in a cave way ahead and way back ...O...at the start & end of the world.

And then the skateboard forms & rushes towards him & before he can run it drifts through him; a startled crushed face against where his face should be.

O...

Moloch:

Almost reveals, to himself, himself.
And then puts that revelation
along with himself
(always himself)
along with his other self
back on the shelf.

Moloch is only one point of who this doctor is & he is
buried close to his own galactic center.
He is so hidden in the chart that he's unaware of such
times when the pencil clicks to make a note, when the lead
breaks & snaps across the page, when he grabs a forty-
wink nap beside the patient's head.

Moloch moves as fast as the clicker of the mechanical
pencil, & hides far behind the past of this doctor's mind –
where he schemes to discover ways to find his ex-wife
leaving the hospital.

Moloch is dreamer of the dreams that vanish when the
doctor wakes with vague memories of mistakes he cannot
recall making, hidden in dreams the doctor never will
remember.

Moloch is there when the Doc is writing, not so much in
the words, as in the power behind the words, where, when
he writes the pencil always breaks the lead.
"How can this pencil always break?" the good Doc
wonders – & from behind his brain, Moloch laughs &
makes sure the pencil lead will snap again.

Snap.

When the whispering doctor awakens beside the bedside of sleeping patients he's filled with rage at writing while asleep. The rage makes his arms and heart catch on fire, carries flames through forests of small clay figures. He is alarmed.

The doc's sleeping hand has written across paper that he must later crumple, or tear in neat lines and cast away. Who wrote this? In my writing? Who wrote this?

His is a hidden life.

While patients nested in comas still sleep he whispers to them the details of his life:

His wife, when she left him (a year ago today) told him, "I truly do not know any one thing about you that could make me stay. You are..." she paused, searching for the right word as if it were behind him at an angular point, "...invisible."

"That's absurd" he whispered aloud, even though he thought "It's good she's going; if she can't see me."

And in the middle of her exasperated sigh, for a moment or two, tears came unbidden, to his eyes.

"I've been a good husband, always calm. Even in our worst of times I believed we got along. I've told you jokes, taken you to the opera, been sometimes witty. What could possibly be wrong?"

"Oh, spirits of the galloping flame – the one that rides high above the sixteen hooves," Moloch roars *"Will he never shut up or stop obsessing about this? May I never sleep? Must I*

always be the observer left awake? How can I possibly, without hurling, bear to hear this all again?"

Just as an example...moments ago just now, you almost cried & so I tried to look inside to figure out if this moment too was real.

All I saw when I looked at the tears, was self-pity.

Whisper that, you shit-head."

Memory tape – of wife leaving: (One Year ago today)

In the coma ward, patient after patient dreams
And to patient after patient
it seems that in all their dreams
the good doctor's words
whisper the same story:
All coffee & no cream.

The doctor's eyes filled with tears again, now real, but too late for him to reveal his true heart. The Cab had arrived & his wife had started (carrying her own suitcase) out the door. She'd let herself through the little gate he'd painted red, in contrast to the white picket fence, so clean and gleaming in the moon.

In their months apart he fully believed that his heart had no need to grieve her leaving; that somehow she'd deceived him at the beginning of their years together. That, even in Med school, the late night prep for exams together, the chocolate treasures he'd hidden at Easter, when he left clues glued to the walls of their small apartment, the years inside a bigger house, with no room for an Easter bunny, or jokes or fun – he'd come to believe, in retrospect, that she'd always planned to leave – each winter when they shared hot chocolate, the x-rays in that spring they'd scanned together looking for what might be hidden in the shadows they checked together...The..."

He stops. His heart hurts so much he cannot revisit memory – open up its door once more. His memory, once upon someone else's time, his greatest treasure, now brings him only pain.

Eventually, he manages to forget. He forgets that she'd ever slept beside him; on a distant autumn day had wed him, witnessed by their friends from Med school. He forgets that at his stag he fell and cut a trench into one eyebrow. His friends sewed it with bright blue thread and he had tiny, perfectly-tied, suture bows to greet his wedding day. "You get to be the *something blue*" they laughed. And in those days he laughed. Laughter was a waterfall inside his chest, beneath his aching head.

When he didn't know, in all the laughing, was that his bride was the "something borrowed."

He forgets his wife was once his lover, had over the years, shared a dozen smiles or two, had always been as calm as he, had never fought on any occasion, had puzzled over people who fought and bled and hurt and yelled – had never been surprised, had never surprised him until the night she left him and their bed.

He talked with others about her until he drove his friends mad, past the point of boredom, of how she was still a gifted surgeon. How she could repair a shattered brain with such sure hands. Why even that old man who had been tugged from a bottle by a speeding train now could, after the knife of his ex-wife, construct, with skill and luck simple sentences could, when prompted, remember who he was.

This doctor, the doctor who has forgotten his ex-wife & their years together, had always been called the king of memory because he'd remembered all so well, could reproduce a printed page years after reading it word for word, comma after comma, rendering into sleeping ears to link coma after coma: thru sleeping dreams still be picture perfect, still render the print exactly as it lay upon the page.

He could recall the pain of each minute of a broken ankle when he was a child, the way the flowers in his sickroom smelled. He recalled each horse-race he'd been to with his gambling father; the way his father would start to scream: "You four-legged bastards run! Run! Pick up the pace!!!" and throw his winning ticket twirling in the air just in time so that it vanished just before it hit the floor.

In short, the doctor who hid Moloch in his shadow, could remember all.

But now memories glide away; will not stay, they fall and shatter. This doctor discovers he can no longer remember, her face when he looks away. His eyes look downward to the ground if she walks by in the exercise yard. He's come to understand that this is as it should be. 'Normal' he believes this is; the ideal situation.

Sometimes she does nod 'hello' & though his eyes are sometimes turned towards her he can swear she does not, ever, see him as he nods. His ex makes of the hospital quadrangle a prison exercise yard when she avoids his look. It's as if they are distant convicts, lifers, their minds linked to calendars with Xs stroked across the days.

His mind's great powers are now directed to a more shadowed puzzle. Why does he wake up suddenly to see pages filled with the insane scribblings of a stranger?

He prays that his world will never, ever, change again. The doc believes all will return, past current danger, to the way that things were meant to be. The scribbles gone, his ex-wife melted, smeared across a page. Wiped away from memory like a sponge tossed on a bonfire.

Despite all that, the knocking on wood, the avoiding stepping on cracks, keeping his fingers crossed behind his back, his memory slips and falls.

Gabriel's Dark Moon:

Soon waxing into silver birth
revealing Gabriel spinning
beneath the Earth.

Gabriel is falling; falling into his full true name, past memories of who he used to be, a childhood recollection of his mother reading to him about Alice – a song fragment, "One sip makes you little ...." his mother's face & then the first time he dropped acid, the network of the veins inside his hand, the pools of light leaking in drops inside his eyelids dripping tears down his amazed cheeks & reflected in a mirrored mirror that he climbed through. He thought he could escape – all was so clear. Pity he hadn't chosen a private place to do this. When they caught him, when they 'observed' him – well, things haven't been the same since.

Although none of this is new to him (the thoughts have occurred to him before at many times) he is surprised to observe his thoughts fly by him in the tumbling "I've-fallen-into-a-hollow-tree-falling-arse-over-teakettles-in-the-dark."

It is not by a change in air that he senses the endless drop ending, nor by a shift of light (for it has grown darker and darker.) Instead he tastes it by a pressure on his chest, a band that constricts movement, & when he senses this pressure the darkness begins to lift and though he still continues to fall like a trans-gendered Alice, it's now sideways-floating: more comforting somehow. Tipped and tilting towards the light he does not want the light.

He has dined enough on light, he wants to taste the spindrift from this new dark flight. He's grown fond of the dark, of the speed of falling, while seeing flying images from random thoughts projected against the inside of his eyelids.

-::- Flash -::-

Boom!
Snap!
Crackle!

"Rice Krispies" he thinks, as his ears hear more than rushing air. "I must remember this," he thinks – "...how to get back to the falling, the field, the path, the tree, the hollow at the base of the tree, the dark. I must never forget this. I'm going to hold this memory of..."

He cares no more about forgetting his multiplication tables, nor how to spell 'parallel,' nor which wines are good or bad, white or red. Gabriel is prepared to forget the smell of his grandmother's kitchen, the scent she created with an infusion in oil of lilac; the way he soiled himself in public when he was fifty-five, the way it felt to be alive on Independence day when he was ten. The way that life again & again went to pieces pretty much every day from the time that he was born – he will forget all this.

"But" he tells himself as he places these memories on the galloping shelves of the dark walls, "I will give up all this if only I remember how it feels to fall."

Suddenly there's another band of pressure over his thighs & then his ankles. His wrists hurt. He cannot lift his arms & the smell is no longer of sweet rotten wood, of earth-threading-tendrils of white fungus. Instead, the cutting edge of Lysol, fresh on the greenish mist of florescent, stabs in his eyes and out his nose.

Staring in horror, he knows he has been nabbed again.

Instead of falling down, he's falling sideways, strapped to a flying gurney & rolling down a hallway where the ceiling is of rushing falling flying acoustic tiles. He sees a madman in a white coat rushing along, with his aluminum clipboard in shadow. Gabriel yells for help but people only look at him and smile.

He's lost fields, forests, mountains, the breeze, trees, sunshine & cigarette-smoke clouds. And though he has managed to flee all this before; has many times before found heaven in the dark, he's now skidding past the flashing lights of a hospital.

Moloch, with the shaded clipboard; with death in his eyes, leans over, clicks his pencil, breaks the lead & whispers,

"Ah, wandering Gabriel, welcome back from the dead."

The Making of the Sea:

Hardly is this the ocean; this considered curve of blue-black against blackness.

The *End Of Project* sign at the end of the road has stopped the rest of the world from projecting as effectively: it's as if the old *So-Kay* projector had blown the bulb, fried the film, burned the snaking belt and the screen saw only *Ghost Riders in the Sky* fragments of celluloid projected & floating down from the balcony to the audience at the old St. John's Capitol Movie house. And everyone looks up in amazement as it rains fire, as only light projects.

That effective.

The only thing missing is the ocean.

All children make their way past the steaming black soil that contains endless embedded Easter Island rocks. All seven of the seven-year-olds line up dots of light to moor the ocean. Two dots (the furthest apart dots) blink like Morse code filtered through Grendel's mom.

She is at the edge of what should be the ocean, and she's just one small part of Sedna, one fragment of Sedna's endless dream. All await Sedna. She's been swimming since she tumbled through bloody water and watched the departing kayak. "Hell of a way to become a goddess," was her receding thought, until the ocean squeezed her against the shoreline. Some many worlds ago, many oceans ago. The Matinee version of the world.

The children stare at the sweeping edge, the crescent cut of the shore & as they look closer, they see pupils of two eyes, and as they project vision on the water's screen, the blink-blink-blink of those eyes, sends messages to their hands. And all of them, at the all-at-once of stopped time, do look towards each other – eye to eye to eye to eye.

And all listen, nautilus-ear to nautilus-ear becoming the hollow beads through which they thread like an awl the sound of a giant woman's song.

O…

…their mouths move in one word: *Sedna*. Because there is air the ear can hold the word & they chant, "Sedna, Sedna, Sedna."

O…

…She, the giant captured in a tightened noose of light, hears back her name, and lifts her head ever so slightly from her pillow of fingers beneath the crescent sea; fingers cut & churned & laced. Her back becomes the reef/ the coral/ the crusted anchor of other lives.

Her vertebrae of old galleons, kayaks, canoes, rafts, debris, pop-bottles from other far off past lives, begin to stretch. The ocean grows, spreading into and through the darkness; through and past the light & the earth, new land, new found land, now shudders with her every move, and starts smoking; smoking all round the tiny feet of all the children.

"Sedna. Sedna, Sedna."

Her legs kick out: liquid legs & black earth legs & stone kneecap legs, and theirs is no longer a slice of water, but is water herself in a grain of rice, the drop of water holds an ocean or seven or one.

"Children", she calls. "O. Eve. Children's Eve."

And then, only then when she hears Sedna's voice (as sure as there's a man in a midnight blue jacket) does Eve let what is to happen truly happen. Again. Now. Start. Beginning. End. Landmark on the equator. Cooked by the expanding sun. It is time.

Eve feels her ribs pop open, and she remembers her name, her village, her peopling of the world and she stands and grows, uncoiling, as long as a page of foolscap, a scroll. Giving birth to the first man, her hand reaches up and Eve's fingers glow with light and on this night she writes scarlet on rice, with one of Sedna's fingers:

S

Sedna, kicks her legs across the world & they curve & flood the earth & the earth cups her legs. And she boils the land to crust and it cracks like crème Brule & the sky-crust becomes her cluttered floor, and she readies to stand.

- O...

...the mighty roar, the squalling, pop-pop-pop of her voice, the whiskers of her words, the fins her fingers make; the gills, the scales, as they swim in her.

Her cave expands and then births all water: the copper-hued water, the aqua, the ultramarine, the blood-blue waves, the reds & browns & yellows & golden orbs & green & purple kelp & man o'wars, & O's eggs with spikes, and she swims in herself, rises from herself.

O, she swims. Her legs kicking, churning.

E

Every ripple becomes a wave, each wave goes rogue, and curls, widdershins, unto and of itself.

D

Down, deeper and deeper. As she dives, more colours pour towards the lands. Over the lands.

N

Now the boys approach, and all along the beach, the black goes beige, turns white, pink, blue; is covered in the hair of kelp & sea-urchin-combs are there & when all the boys walk into her waves, they find they can breathe water.

Their necks open and they are rock tumbled, ocean boiled. Blood pouring from their gills, they fill kelp bubbles, bubbles detach fish float. Warm blood cold. Blood.

A

Arrow appears at the door of Sedna's eyes, and is tossed like a beach ball from another life to this new one, with a piece of wood beneath his feet. He grips, with talon-toes, the wood, and surfs along her kelping hair to comb that hair. He's combing out the past, the Javex bottles, driftnets, graduation helium balloons & dragger trawls, the hooks, the harpoons, the dead whale bones, the debris that takes a coral age or two to gather and to be released.

Ravens fly through the dark sky & lift the debris.

They angle & slip & circle Pele's volcano & from the earth they foam as she presses down the earth & water boils & all follow each other into the crackling Sedna sea. Combers of flame.

The burning of all this is eaten by the air.

And eye-to-eye, Arrow bows, rises to the surface & on a wave that works a platformed hand without her fringes - he is dropped to the beach.

She cries with relief as the last of the debris leaves her untangled hair. Her tears are of stone, of new-born Adamite, of granite, Labradorite, & Moukalite, hot & cold crystals, citrine & all do beach-glass drop onto the new sand just as Arrow is dropped & skates upon them like a skateboard on marbles.

Suddenly there are trees, and suddenly the trees are rolled & the pumiced rocks carve more Tiki faces & the flames are singing.

A giant wave carries Arrow in her fingerless hand & drops him on the pebbled rush & marble-rattles back to the ocean. Whoosh...

...Whoosh...whoosh...

and Arrow...

......is home at last.

Luna Di Luna:

Touches the Sliver Of The Moon
with her mind and finds
Inside her singing chest

Everything she needs to find.

Peeled from the moon, one lunar sliver spirals through night into the ocean; phosphorescent green ghostly glow is trailing light along the littered beach. The first quarter moon sheens discarded condoms, a dead seagull, empty beer cans & soda bottles rolling & bumping into pilings of downtown piers. Into the light walks Luna, fully clothed, her arms upraised.

"Grandmother Moon, who brought me here to kiss your Pacific waves – though you are nearly hidden from my eyes you're clear as day inside my heart. Your beating heart is home to Luna di Luna. Know when I commend myself into your glow-in-the-dark cluttered waters I trust what you may give."

Although Seattle holds bright lights and plenty of stores and restaurants, places filled with music and with booze, she pays them no notice whatsoever. Luna has not come here to mix with the hip, the debonair, she has no wish to meet the urban folk, the intelligentsia who fill cafes with their views; whose words spill over beaches into the ocean.

Luna knows as she waits for the answer of the moon that it will, no matter what, be securely connected to Mother Ocean, to lights twinkling from houseboats that creak at ends of moorings. A black Labrador dog, mouth triumphantly gripping a stick, swims towards her. The dog & the stick are outlined in the light bouncing on Pacific water.

But that's not what catches her eye. What makes her breath catch & her heart skip, what makes a sigh of astonishment escape her lips, is what's tangled in the stick: fishing line with green slime hung along it like Alien washing strung to dry, leading to a floating log.

On that log lies the gift of Eve; the seashell nestled in the hollow of the wood, the golden glitter and purple swell of the abandoned purse. The rays of the moon do angle new planes across the log's face. 'Tiki Log,' she thinks.

The dog swims towards Luna di Luna; the line detaches & the log sinks low in the ocean, turning, turning. The shell drifting to the edge of a singing wharf. When Luna di Luna clambers down she takes the purse & opens the purple clasp to see the cash that Eve had stuffed inside the purse.

She turns her eyes upwards to the sky & to the edge of the lunar shawl.

"I thank you. This will pay for what my instincts tell me to do. All of us – sisters and brothers – will gather near the waters of Seattle to wait. I will do exactly what it is that you tell me I must do. Whatever it may be."

She slings the wet purse over her shoulder.

Across the city, inside a blazing hospital, Eve looks towards the ocean, & turns to touch the Orderly on the shoulder.

"Thank you for considering my request about the garden. But before you plow up the narrow hall, to seek beneath it such a cherished garden on hallowed ground I must tell you that somewhere else, within this sacred city, my seeker has been found."

Sedna is swimming, she is the ocean, her hair is untangling.

She looks over the waves. And time-wind blow as she sings. To & fro. Back & forth.

O...

...Time winds.

Luna Di Luna:

Luna di Luna, the former Music Girl,
locates the first part of her puzzle.

Her second day in the city of Seattle & Luna wanders past Pike Place Market. A good night's sleep in the park, her cash-plugged purse snuggled near her belly button. No one bothered her till the very end of the first night, when a skinhead-retro-wannabe reached out to touch the dew upon her electrified hair. The smirk upon his face disappeared when Luna grabbed him by the neck.

"Listen to me, balding boy. You must learn not to toy with a girl who sleeps in the park. I am Luna. By day, the Sun guards me & in deep night I am protected by moonlight. Even if I were all alone on an earth without a string of lights hung on a nearby sky I could defend myself by my own true left hook and right."

Retro-boy chokes out a brief apology while disintegrating into the foliage, his swagger gone, his style that of a slinking dog; of an upset toad upon a slippery rolling log that tumbles, with a sinking sucking sound, into a deep bog where there's only the sound of that plunging log. Luna looks to the sky and knows that she is safe.

Hungry she is for breakfast, though she does not want to use her miracle cash – that's for something more amazing than the smell of crabs in boiling water grabbing her by the nose; the lilt of fresh sourdough. Tightening her belt, she decides to move on, her hopes already floating on the ocean, her mind filled with planks and resin, tar and twine – until she hears a piano & her heart tells her to run back to the market, for , although the work of someone who is certainly not a hack, it's a creation of arpeggios & trills, like Mozart mixed with Liberace & filtered through Frank Mills. What pulls her through Seattle is the sound of the piano itself!

O...

...That's what tugs her; lodestone-pulled from inside a magnet. Around the stalls and booths she goes until she finds a huge, dazzling, green Grand Piano beneath a glittering sign that reads, "Grand Thomas and his Green Grand. Stand and listen so your soul, itself, may be grand."

There's no doubt that Thomas is Russian. In his white waistcoat and white tails, his hair curls Zamphir-style beyond his bony shoulders. He is Thomas Zarov. He has a massive Cossack mustache. His cheeks are thin and gaunt, his eyes self-trained to smolder, do smolder, making widows cover him with flowers and vanilla as he coaxes the piano into a Bizarro Franz Liszt series of runs and spills. Pleased with himself, he smiles to see the glass goblet on his piano fill with crinkled bills.

He smiles through a storm of red roses thrown by his biggest fan, an eagerly-awaiting-anything & yet, unrealized, widow. Thomas makes flamboyant bows towards the land and then the Pacific, but when he turns around he sees - to his amazement - that a sandy-haired, pale, freckled-faced, girl is seated at his piano.

The rose-flinging widow is outraged & truth to tell, so is Thomas. This redhead at his green piano has taken over *his* stage. His rage begins to build until her hands ripple over the keyboard.

He stops his lunge towards the keyboard and listens, blood freezing in fright. His marrow turns to ice as she plays for him, his childhood. Her long-fingered hands in blue & grey cut-off gloves, playing memories of his Leningrad nights and days, his tiny hands tickling the giant keyboard of a battered Baby Grand, might as well be rippling along his spinal keyboard.

She *knows* he hates his teacher & so, she plays for Thomas the scent of tallow candles in cheap lofts. In a rush and blur of fingers, flashing, dancing, leaping; she follows him with slamming notes as he trudges up to lessons in old-school Commie buildings where the lifts are always locked. She plays for him the way he heard Chopin's inner song that must be played in secret (like words never spoken)

She coaxes from his piano, Thomas' fantasies of America & those late-nites when his fingers played anything by George Gershwin. Floating over the Pacific, in a mist of music, she fills clouds with his journey to New York, the Cruise Lines' closing curtain, the fall from grace until he began to play only what people thought they wished to hear, the way he never, ever, played for himself any more. Instead of all that wall-to-wall, she slams into Rachmaninoff playing a Chopin prelude. This ain't YouTube; the sound shakes him & fills his ears. It shakes his bones & opens his ears & eyes & heart. You know: a gift wrapped in black & white.

What he hears, hidden in her music, are the nights he cried himself to sleep, tossing & turning because his talent sat with back turned towards his heart. When she finishes playing, he understands he's been tossed another start & knows that if he gives away his piano & sells all he's come to own, he may stand once again, anew – why, then he'll discover what his true talent may do.

"My piano?" he yells to Luna, "It's a gift for you!"

She leaps and hugs him with a whoop.

"I'll deliver it today" he smiles & then he gives a laugh as she tells him when the time comes she wants it lugged to the ocean & placed upon a raft she's meant to build – a round raft of exotic & familiar wood!

Their hands lift above the Piano Grand & music floats to sea, as they play together & his childhood hands from Russia join hers in finding what must be played.

See the two of them together, eyes looking out to sea; hearts linked to the piano, hands together in a blur. There is only Luna and Thomas.

Then there's only music.

Finally, only the sea.

Moloch:

The dream of Moloch brings him something new.
While a reading of his dream by the good doctor
begins to show him precisely what he is to do.

"Moon in Pisces, solitary in the twelfth house" a fortune-teller said, once upon a time, to the shadow of the good doctor as he tried to push past her, on his one and only visit to Venice Beach, inside the past century's turn.

He'd already put up with dogs in kerchiefs, had spurned young men with oiled Pecs, avoided murals that offended his cultivated taste & reluctantly administered first-aid to roller-bladers who'd had the good fortune to upend next to him. He'd even dealt with his someday-to-be-ex-wife, clapping and hooting, "Don't you love this vacation?!"

She'd put her hands together, oohed and ahhhed, delighting in this scene; not finding any of it odd. And when a youthful woman grabbed him by the sleeve, his wife clapped her hands again, instead of asking her to leave. The good doctor did not see what any fool would, the young fortune-teller was a beautiful woman with eyes of Scorpio blue. He didn't notice her keen chiseled cheekbones, nor her tattooed earlobes. From the left lobe dangled a swelling Venus of Willendorf. All he wanted was for her to leave his sleeve alone.

His wife took a deep breath & put her hands upon his chest.

"How does she know that? About the moon inside your chart? And its position in the twelfth house, dear, how could she know that, when she's never seen your chart?"

"I've not seen it myself!" snapped the good doctor. "She could say I'd been born under the sign of a... stubborn mule and I could not venture a contrary opinion. All I can truthfully say & now I do – is that she and her opinion are all a load of rot."

"It's not," smiled the psychic, "I say, 'Not!' And, by the way, your sun is in the sign of Virgo."

"Oh no. That's so right!" laughed the to-be-ex, slapping the woman on the back.

The good Doctor moved away & the fortune-teller followed him "I have something life-shattering to tell you – I must speak this truth today."

"I haven't anything to give you!"

"That doesn't matter. I've something vital to tell you that I suspect your Virgo nature will not hear. It's an event that will not happen for more than fifteen years. I'm giving this information to the Pisces moon in the twelfth house part of you (by the way, that placement will see you working in an institution)"

"There you're wrong – I'm going to grow rich in private practice."

A hoot. The soothsayer plucks at his sleeve and then follows him, addressing his retreating back.

"In fifteen years you will dream a dream of truth. You and your shadow."

"I know that song" he jokes.

"You and your shadow will dream of three things! Do not laugh!

First, you will see the face of your shadow. When you see this, know you have fallen far from grace.

At that time, you'll also help dream into existence in the world a raft of oddly matched lashed wood, strapped together from fragmented precious trees you will not know by name but that will smell of sap so true and sweet that you'll want to eat this raft like a wooden cookie. You will observe all this only if you awaken from your chosen nap and see a horse grazing *in* a hospital hallway. Blackie will be his name.

The third thing to be, is that you'll hear sweet music from a piano bobbing like a white wave on the ocean. When you hear this, be aware that you must take all who are dancing with you, and board your piano raft.

Set sail on this craft – trusting that the final place you land will be your necessary destination. When you dream this dream it will be time to encounter your great fear – that you have lost your mind. Be kind to your self.

O, just in case I forget to give thanks for rendered alms"
she shouted, "Thank your fine ex-wife, for the gold that
passed from her hand across my outstretched palm."

When the good Doctor's much-better half caught up with
him, he had one question, "Just what did she mean by
calling you my ex-wife?"

"Don't know for the life of me" she smiled & threw her
arm across his shoulders "Let's leave the beach and explore
the bed in our hotel room, before your chart changes."

On his next birthday she gave him a hand-colored chart
that showed his moon in Pisces floating all alone in his
twelfth house. His eyes did not pop in astonishment from
their sockets to see the proof that the fortune-teller had been
right. Instead he thought this was proof that she'd somehow
picked his pocket, read his license & gathered enough
information from there to guess, on a weird whim, his birth
chart. All to get even with him because of his scoffing at
Psychics in Southern California's sandy beaches.

Well, you can see why the good doctor's predicted 'ex-to-
be' left him, & why there were no replacements lined up.

He naps beside Arrow's bed. Sometimes he wakes up,
whispers in the kid's ear. Then drifts off to sleep again.

Moloch awakens first from the fifteen-years-ago
predicted dream that he and the good doctor share. Being
aware that he must set this down before the doc can awake,
he writes:

> "The soothsayer told you so! Read this
> or I will come back and scream in total
> rage.
> You'll look like a embarrassed rabbit in
> a hutch, quivering from the wounds of
> noonday heat. I'll hold you, nailed with
> words & captured on a page!!!"

And on & on he writes in a style guaranteed to get the doc's attention; to make sure he does not merely crumple up the sheet before he's read the content. Slim lengths of mechanical pencil-lead go click, click, click in flight across the clipboard to bounce upon the pure white bed.

He finishes the last word – this time his handwriting clear and neat, just as the good doc jumps to his feet, leaping from his almost forgotten, dreams of deepest sleep.

And reads what he needs to read.

The Lighting of The Fire:

Out of fire comes the wood.
Out of wood comes the ash & charcoal.

Out of the ash & charcoal we all emerge. We are doilies draped over cooling charcoal, burning our way into the coal's shadow. We are the impression of the Trilobite and we are the Trilobite; the shade & the light.

The fire burns now in air. On & of earth. It burns along our arms & over our bellies. It spouts and leaks flames, water, earth & steam from our cave. We are, all of us, first a dot - then a flare to the dot & next a girl & from the girl we then become both boy and girl.

Out of fire comes fire.

It burns foam into waves, candle & wick, burns in our ears, burns out our eyes. Our faces blackened, still we sit, legs folded like pretzel-dough.

Back wavering like a volcanic eruption, as black as an oil spill our ribs smoke like fireplace spills & smoke-burn, and we hold our fiery hand to link with each other as our heads rage away. We sit in this cave in a cloud.

O...

...one giant cloud, the seal of the imprint, floats over the world. And it is the end of the eighth day and the start of the ninth night. We burn, reform, into black and white charcoal beings, and we rise in clouds of many colors. We are the mirror of the world. We are reflected on the mirror of the sea.

Sedna coils the cloud & one by one we rain back to earth. Some parts of us are rocks, more are trees, there are snails, communal community slugs, mushrooms; Ororobus & curled fiddleheads. Spiders, earthworms, cultures seething, centipedes crawling, book lice singing. Us.

A solar flare leaps from the head of the sun to the head of the earth. A lunar pulse oscillates the singing heart of the forest & the two burn in coldness & in lungs & gills, and still we rain.

The rocks in the center of the cave catch eternally into flame. Smoke rises. Newly formed again, we look each other in the eyes. We rain on each other's sooty lids.

And I am Eve. I am Arrow. I am the Man in the Black Jacket with silver stars as buttons. I am Maud. I am Ern. I am Thomas. I am Moloch. I am the Music Girl and Luna de Luna. Stephen Lo. Yemaya. And I am Queen Mab & her faeries of fire, faeries of earth, sylphs of water & of air. I am ideas glowing & burning like the sixth sense spilled unto ash of slate. I am stones & the imprint of our butts on stone. I am snot & slime & leaves & shadow & light. I am fox farts & red teeth & gnawed bones. I am Phonse & Susie, Ariel & Skipper, Skipper Lo & what he chants. I am the phonebook shaken until names fall out.

I am me.
I am fire.
My heart burns.
I am red letters on pale rice.
Still.

Queen Mab:

Expanding the circle of magic
our rites are near complete;
we create, in unison, our circle.
The invocation is sounded.
Your throat throbs its own heartbeat.

Mab chants & the circle chants back.
  "Before the necessary magic, before the invention of background and foreground; O…before the fierce intervention by Descartes between the human & the world, between this world & other worlds; the curled and uncurled, the straight, obvious, blocked & the opened gate – there's the Poem & in the world of poems there is no sin – for every

Grendel has & needs a Beowulf, each desert is matched with water cool; each silence requires its din.

There are no divisions between question & answer, no differences in "Yes, sir" & "No, Sir."

What we know is that "Sir" is the killing point. There's no difference in still Zen point & mere superficial Prancer, between cattle and rancher, between cheap & earned rhyme. In distant time, before the philosopher who rode behind the horse – before Cartesian fake duality there was, in that smoky fog filled time of either-or/no time & we may now & then live in that world: in our natural clime.

It requires something more and less than Arrow & the Music Girl known as Luna, more and less than myself, Queen Mab, or even Yemaya, Moloch, Stephen the Orderly, Gabriel or any of the up-front bunch of characters, what movies would call the 'leads', it needs besides the good Doc or Eve (with lead actress quality hidden up her sleeve) more than the Wild Bunch waving as they leave, it needs – well, if your hunch allows you to greet the driver of the magic blue bus, or a random cab, or the man wearing, at the baseball game, a look-alike Garth Brooks shirt & a blue-black jacket with stars as buttons, or perhaps the mother and the father of Luna, with their fried chicken or chicken-skin sandwiches – if your hunch has you look at them every bit as much as all the others, the protagonists in different schemes, you'll know what I mean when I say all of these people inhabit the same world, all of them dream sections of one very large, puzzle-hooked dream & none of them are 'special.' There are no extras, and we need them all.

If you see this – if you greet all beings in any book & curl their toes (along with yours) while you are reading, or listening to the book being spoken aloud; if you lean back so they become a part of the words in your mind & aren't just part of the crowd, and let your fingers do the reading over dots of word, spines of sentences, then you're with us, Sister! You are with us, Brother, you are with me, with all others. We declare all are welcome here, all beings and non-beings spinning through galaxies near and far.

Welcome to earthworms who will chew our pages & then shit loam so we may grow more trees. Kittens are welcome to claw the corners of this book. Dogs may grab it and sideways crab away, skulking and running away with rectangular paper Frisbees. They may call, if they choose, this book home; may swallow it, crap it out & that's just fine with us.

Death-beetles clicking in the eventual mold left by bookworms, the squirm of larvae blooming, as paper worms do in water, may do so in the ocean inside these pages. And for those who, against the all pervading cold, rip out the pages to burn them in the never-ending winter night – why that's all right. Here, have a light, roll a doob – a fatty with end pages & settle in, blow out the smoke & see, while rising towards the moon, it holds all the faces that this book wears on its sleeve. Welcome all, no need to read or understand, these pages. Just sniff the book, use it as a coaster, rub the shiny cover on your cheek in a cheap hotel room.

No need to remark "Ah, part of the great design."

We do not care if this is mocked, not a bit, if one or more of you says "Is this book crazy? What a piece of shit!" that's just waiting for critics to type it with their bone-weary hands. We welcome all – this is an infinitely expanding hall.

So, as you might suspect, we cannot move along until all who once were in the background, stand front & center & reenter, as we sing along. They all get to, in the fluid of your spine, sing solos. As they do this, hold also this in mind, if you can so balance them in your mind, when they leave the page – and if you keep them as your center focus, please do so. If the man in the Garth Brooks shirt stays with you & you find he strolls into your writing or your idle thoughts & if it seems he wishes to sing *I got Friends In Low Places*, in an off-key-not-quite-successfully-cloned-voice-loaned-to-him-from-the-deep-recesses-of-your-memory-banks…O…– please do enjoy his company, let him sing you into and then out of sleep.

If there are gently rocking Mother Ships, with beings of orange and molten light who shift their ships to fluffy summer clouds, with mind-beams three, or who hum sacred chords without a throat, we welcome all and invite you to take inside your ship, this book.

Place it next it to those alien classics you carry with you, that remind you of what you know as your Blue-Planet home. This is such a huge hall that we (myself included) find we cannot, alone, hold it in our spider-web-linked small mind. No matter what we do, there's room a-plenty for what you sing, or do not sing. The Music Girl needs us. We are the true movie extras of this world's big film; her secret musical treasure.

Let us sing our devotion to the moon and sun & every orb of every world that ever has or ever will exist including those we have not thought of – for how could we – we are not gods & goddesses. We are, all of us, nothing special. Cigarette butts under not so special heels. O..yes…that's fine. The way we all hold Buddha in our guts, is the same way we all hold Jane and John Doe, and Jane & Jane, and John & John. In our minds, we are kith and kin beneath and on the surface of our skin.

Hear the song of this mixed dream born of winter and of fall, of summer and of spring, see all of us link hands to make this book become a raft, to hold all that we have thought to bring."

And, for the nonce, finished, Mab dances the rest of the words. Her feet are mix-master blades at full throttle, eyes are pin-wheels. Brows smoke.

Up and down the walls, across the floor, big black boots blooming from beneath her robes, she spins until she rises into the air, spins and spins some more, and thuds with her egg-beater feet until she splinters the locked door.

"Poem Matrix!" she screams & no one cares.

Poem Matrix" she screams and leaps, once more, into the air,

&
nobody cares

&
everybody cares.

The building of the Buildings

Maud & Ern are old again. And all the children gather round, now tired from the building of the necessary world. But know there is one more thing to do.

And so they invent the wheel.

All lie down upon the beach, and the sand they've gathered is warm & holds their bodies much better than memory's foam. Crown of head to crown of head, foot to foot - the rim of wheel. All around a circle.

"Eve," says Ern, "it's time to dream."

"Eve," says Maud, "dream your special dream."

And as she does, it threads the circle, links minds, till, sleeping, they begin to build a town. The town that burned down in those dreams in Hollywood, when Eve, sleeping-mask like video goggles on a snowboarding fool flies down the impossible slope, up & down, turns & slams around in a dream-town, knees absorbing the shock of crashing home & being swept through the town she dreams of when she's grown up.

At first all fingers twitch when she remembers the blasty boughs catching fire from her fast-typing fingers. Sparks are still blowing flames around the town, around the white picket fences of her dreams. All see the orange & Vermillion splashes, the salmon belly timbers resting on a smoky knoll.

But then, they dream the snow. And as it hits the flames, it absorbs the heat, and makes an ice palace outport, with white picket fences, parlour windows, inside the homes pump frosty pump organs, mice chew sheet music nests, attics fold old copies of *Lilliput* Magazines. The *Gerald S. Doyle Bulletin's* playing on the radios & there are church suppers & there are men smoking outside the lodges & there are, once again, boats in George's Cove.

And all forms anew – right behind the Mockingbird Motel, where, finally – the neon tubes return to glowing over snow which goes purple and green.

And then our sleeping dreams expand, and begin to hold the world. Past, present, future – all click rotating bands, and Istanbul returns to Turkey, Italy reforms and Rome arrives. In India, Friday phantoms gather at Dhaak Wali Ziarat with Dhaak Wale Peer. There's Carbonear in Terra Nova & there's a place without a name in Siberia where a herder tones an image of sleeping children & a cave forms in his pulsing throat. His tones place my table, red chair and microscope as defined & in Lapland as firm as a reindeer's hoof in snow. Hoof-prints sound in an empty room for, in this time-wind, I am gone & as I am, the room is empty once more, until a film crew comes looking for a location of despair, of emptiness. So, the room's, once again, empty.

There's every place you've ever heard of, all the stories you've been told, the TV shows, the Movies, the gum you stepped in at the prom, or stuck under a seat at the old *Majestic* cinema. First love, last love. First date's house. Last date's house. There's medals & gold stars & old bongs & posters for movies you've never seen.

The sky snows letters, and notches in wood, nail-prints in clay & runes & all the words of the world are & were & will be snowing down, dust-storming through the desert.

All at once.

All of us.

Now & forever.

And also there's nothing. Holding it all in infinite space, where we grow and spin and die…

…O…

…all settles – just as it is when you woke up this morning.

All the same.

For now.

Queen Mab Speaks again

Speaks so she may, as Queen Mab,
welcome all Pilgrims
even those of little or no faith.
She's in no hurry.
& knows we are a ragged lot
She ain't Chaucer, and this ain't Canterbury
She's not even Queen Guinevere
Though this may become our Camelot.

"This is" observes Queen Mab "an auspicious moment. Time for us to plan our world. Poem-matrix, kids. Unencumbered by 'true' memories, we stand naked, which allows us, boys and girls, to link & unlink arm in arm with *Knowledge*.

Not the kind embedded in our snapshots, taught in college, the stories our teachers told of the transmutation of lead into gold, in any sort of metaphorical, alchemical way, nor is this an echo of all the unreal lives we were so scared to leave, that each time we were trapped - we called it victory.

'Tis a different place – for this is Queen Mab's Great Hall & Maud & Ern's cave, where all of us may be exactly who we wish to be. We punch precise pedants out, leave participles dangling, spell parallel with twenty 'l's" , we run away with readers for a weekend's worth of fun, find ourselves pregnant when a month has run, and our sentences await a period

Instead of fleeing, we walk into the mouth of the very large, very old crocodile & floss her creaking teeth with the string taken from a banjo that we've hidden in a purse.

Then that crocodile eats us & leaves our shoes. Or spits out just the buckles into Ruckle Park.

Let me introduce myself – for I am Queen – and if you look in the corner of the room, what may be, by the keen observer, seen upon a Gurney tilted up, hidden by the shadows from the curtains is our King – King Arrow - who will, this night, take a bow. Your fame in this Great Hall is always certain. For an hour or two, anyhow. I'm a king. You're a queen. Anyone who reads this, I say to you, 'Hi your majesty.' Yeah, that's the aristocracy – the all of us. No fuss.

Hereeeee's King Arrow."

Arrow takes no bow. He lies, as if in state, upon his Gurney. Burnished tubes of metal are curved to hold the folds of a worn hospital blanket. William Blake could sit and sketch, in the early etching of learning, but if he did, he'd see this is no El Cid; the kid's a living king, his crown is in his heart, his heart is in the Milky Way, just like the rest of our long lost tribe. He's meant to get up & seize the diem.

"It's fate" says Yemaya "that you should talk & tho' I'm sorry, it's also fate that this boy cannot walk."

However, Meg has stopped. Her eyes glaze over, her jaw dips. The nurse stops and sighs. Mab slips away, head surrendering to the grip of gravity, inclining to the right. Fate has stepped in once again and turned out (as the old joke will have it) the porch light.

Yemaya expects to hear no more from Mab that night. Lost words unravel on the floor. Drool wets the word yarn on the carpet.

The Nurse had hoped for more; would trade her uniform for more & would erase some of her own favorite recollections to see this woman's eyes unglaze, jaw grow firm...O...to see just one patient learn something new, stand in the middle of the room with at least one memory that tests sure. She wants to see one new dog learn old tricks so she can enter the miracle in the logbook of the floor of memory.

Both she and Stephen Lo have ended up official greeter for all the guests who've come to stay. This duo, who've told doctors and administrators to 'Kiss My Ass', believe deep in their souls, that the boulder which blocks recall may be one day unrolled from the mouth of recollection's cave. That, one magic night, every patient who has gathered in this great cave will remember.

That's why each night they join whisperers all over the world who go up to those who cannot hear, and who share, once more *sotto voce*, story after story; share secrets, heap praise, tell jokes, sing days and nights, draw symbols over sleeping souls, roll invisible smokes for them, listen as if we're hearing our jokes told back to us, talk to corpses, hear confessions from the dead, see reflections of our dads and moms long after they are buried; supposed to be dead and gone – they're tucked away in secret pillars of our echoing caves. The lost tribe of whisperers climbing into our waiting dreams..

Stephen knows what Yemaya is thinking.

Moving towards Mab he holds her by the arm & gently leads her from her self-chosen dais. If he has a bias it's towards a miracle of golden light, for he believes the brain is only one small part of memory's domain.

Though he's never shared his theories with the Medics, he understands that memory's loss is caused by too much TV, Radio, MP3s, too many newspapers & magazines, by ads selling things and the massing of supposed wealth & the growth-after-growth of *things* themselves. The shelves of stores are blocked with *things* & the words being used to describe those *things* are multitudinous & plastered on billboards near and far, glued on doors, platitudinously written on rooftops, put on packages, used to scroll along the bottom of tiny and large screens, used as credits for people working in movies, printed all over greeting cards, posted on backyards to warn of pretend attack dogs, used in junk mail, painted across what should be pure white canvas sails, written on hockey rink's boards to lure the buyers from around the globe. Blabbing to sell blabbing. Not blogging – just blabbing.

All this is junk & with so much glut, the strain to hold these *things* in memory-place (all caused by those with gold to gather even more gold) and golden time. Stephen knows there's no room left in memory, no more space for thoughts. Too many neurons hold too many pictures. All tied up, they can't do what they're meant to do – breathe freely, sing together. Linked eye-to-eye.

Indeed, his hunch tells him that cancer is caused by the body's frantic search for places to store the excess of things broadcast by this belief in old, familiar gold-I-want-more-gold-O- mommy-daddy-mommy-daddy-I–want-more-gold-baby-wants-more-gold!. That bunch of baby gold-diggers, are able endlessly to discuss gold over business breakfasts and lunches.

Hit me with the mineral water, mother.

Objects are released like a swarm of chiggers to rush the body. And broadcasting TV, Radio, Radar, cell-phones, Internet Viruses all permeate the body & the mind until the sheer weight of all there is to learn, to filofax, to day-timer-enter, to phone home about, to click on the internet & buy and sell – not give but get, & fill the mind with *things* to buy & to tweet & beep & weep & write advertising slogans across the sky for & to make small children cry at Christmas for what they cannot get & give the rich their feather beds, while the poor are led to street corners & pointed towards the waiting grates and told, "If you sleep over this, my friend, why the heat will be just great for you and for the kids."

"How to build slaves" is a very easy-to-read manual.

And the rich believe it does nothing to give a quarter to the panhandler. So they give nothing.

The poor, if so-non-quartered, will cease to believe in the rich & will hang about all year & their wails will affect sales – well, the mixture of all this fills the mind and body to the plimsoll line of memory, and that's supposed to be just fine."

All over the city, throughout all lands, so many *things* to hold inside are killing everyone, thinks Stephen. He knows it's killing off memory & people, speeding up the end.

Although he keeps these thoughts pretty much to himself, he does share them with Yemaya who will be, forever, his dear friend. She nods her great head. And allows as how her world has filled with other's thoughts & if she buys something she wonders sometimes, oftentimes, if it's a good brand, when everyone throughout all lands, knows there's no such thing as a good brand - most things are junk, just the way they're designed to be. She'd read about the Luddites and knows they were on to one of the best thoughts of any century. And Yemaya also knows that if there's too much memory, it stores itself as cancer.

They both whisper this to all people on their ward. Sometimes they see toes twitch. Hey, maybe something will happen. So they whisper some more. Night after night after night. Into ear-caves.

They whisper deep into the day.

Yemaya knows that those in this hall have simply turned *it* off – sensing that it was wearing out, shed the skin of memory – moved past the web of associations – gone within to find a certain stillness. Stopped new storage areas from blossoming into malignant bodies, escaping what's killing us and all nations.

So they think, but do not speak aloud.

And then: this night, from the back, a sudden groan.

And another & Arrow is seen sitting up, like a time-lapse-in-reverse of a wilted flower, thru backwards time, wavering and gaining height. Time-wind blow across the ward.

Yemaya and Stephen stop talking, stop thinking. Heads tune, and Arrow wavers to a sitting position.

All it takes for Arrow to waver awake is to forget about his head; in one nano-second to stop thought & let the pain, scrapes, pins, bolts, metal stitches, plastic stitches, metal head-circle speed away, following the head like the small cars hooked to a runaway engine. The way an Acme magnet activated by Wile E. Coyote may lift a battle-cruiser or suck a satellite into a desert canyon.

Then, it feels as if his head is a pink & white balloon & the pins, like magician's needles thrusting through the skin, find nothing. Next a hiss, and air blows round the room, balloon after balloon, all bursting & deflating until things speed up when, deep inside the pink & white head, more starts to pop.

Pop.

Pop.

Pop...pop...pop.

His head hangs like a pathetic failed birthday gift for Eeyore.

The first part of his head to go is the memory of his forehead, the way he could see his brows when he dreamed above his body, the old friend in the mirror, ready for life's first tattoos. His head nods like a dashboard Elvis. Spring ahead; fall back. As his head began to vanish, he seems supported somehow on the string of drool that made it to his navel. It stretched in half, frayed like an old rope and then broke. He could see his hand arched like an albino spider & as his head is melting, the spider legs turn into Arrow's fingers.

Where his eyes used to be there's now only sight. Time-wind & his hand moved, index finger turned and pointed at himself.

A time back, before the accident, Arrow always has been like a commercial where the parts of an auto engine exploded outwards, so he could see all the bone-engine parts still working, tho' separate. It was like that with his head: the Maxilla bone expanding outwards, teeth and all, flying into space, the Zygomatic bone springing outwards and across the room, and his mandible dropping to the floor, everything expanding.

Disassembling, each bone seen from inside, held in space like floating teacups, white and red, cupped to hold light, and then even those pictures go, he's left with the room.

Period.

Full Stop.

Start up.

Stop.

Starting again – the brain catches. The crank keeps turning.

The room. Just as it is – Yemaya moving ever so slowly, Stephen turning, bit by bit, thru space.

From the empty space where his head was, even the Sphenoid bone has left its perch of bone, and flapped two Pterodactyl wings, going, going...

...Gone through the window. Through the growing space the sound grows, echoes, pings. From where his neck once grew he could feel a roar begin.

The roar burns his throat.

He tries to close his mouth and the sound moves back down his chest like fire. With nothing between him and the world, he hears & heard & will hear, wind whistle over root-bound tumbling teeth. He was & is & will be able to scream three words.

Luna di Luna, is what he screamed.

As Stephen & Yemaya run across the ward towards him, he screams once more, and memory comes to visit where his head had been. He can see and hear his father in his usual breakfast hobby of farting and quoting from the bible. "The Mouth..." Fart. "...That speaketh..." Fart. "...with no tongue." Extended fart.

He can hear his father in the spaces where his ears once heard his father's voice; his father's drunken laugh.

And Arrow smiles. If he'd had a mouth left, it would creak.

And just as Stephen places his left hand on Arrow's right shoulder and, as Yemaya places her right hand on his left shoulder, a picture arrives for Arrow.

Hands over a piano's keyboard, pale stretched fingers: rising towards a red-head's rising in the morning sky, he looks into his dream and sees Luna at her green piano. And he begins to sing & time trips sideways, sucking time-winds behind it.

"True!" calls Arrow "Stephen Lo, the truth is out! In here we may witness heads that are so crammed with shit, they must grow mutant cells. We have all thrown away memory because we're tired of its incessant yells!"

It's Stephen's time to lurch around, his jaw's turn to drop. Knowing his thoughts are revealed.

Yemaya stands, arms folded & a chill wind gusts into the hall. The door strains against the hinges, sensing Grendel is arriving to pick up a few petrified souls. To munch on arms & legs for lunch, rush down the hallway chewing on memory stored in meat.

"You spoke" is all Yemaya says.

"He spoke, indeed, " says Stephen.

"All thought he was brain-dead," muses Eve, her voice both clear & even.

Arrow lunges to his feet. Peter-Boyle-style, with Gene Wilder eyes. He stands, he creaks, he walks, bolts all over the fucking place, the lights hissing and sparking, and the boy walking.

"Has he eaten of the forbidden fruit? Has he slept beneath the tree of knowledge where all becomes crisp as an autumn apple?" Asks Eve.

"The only reason it was forbidden was because we were meant to seek-and-find the apple. To be meek enough to go crazy, to taste its sweet, sweet, core."

"Perhaps we should tell the doctors..." Stephen hesitantly remarks, looking towards the door.

"No!" says Yemaya, "They'll hook him up to even more wires. They'll poke scopes up his ass. They'll strap him in restrains and roll him like *Pork Mushu* in a sheet. They'll also say we're lying through our teeth.

Perhaps, it's time to eat the apple?"

"Yes" says Gabriel "And never tell scientists nor doctors, for they are the Proctors of acculturated thought."

"Holy fuck, he speaks, too!" says Stephen. And Gabriel continues, "If you tell such things to those in charge they will not suddenly see the light; turn over a new leaf & they, sure as shit, will only bring us grief."

All around the hall, Meg, Eve, Arrow himself (head or no head) & the Nurse & Stephen nod. Yemaya smiles and says "We're not to tell, 'cause they'll discount this in their journals & shoot our friends full of crap, plunging them back into the nap that they were taking."

Finally all eyes move to Arrow & see behind him the door of the Great Hall as it trembles.

Arrow slams a hand against the door. Somehow his hand is stained with red ink. He slams again and again. His right hand (a hand that was supposed never to rise again) hits. His left hand smashes, and the wood holds the dents of his knuckles. He, like a mummer on acid, out-breathes into the frosted air.

"No!" he shouts "for someone (not a Savior) is coming to save us all. This is a person just like us; who sees clearly, who makes no fuss about their gifts, who simply...does what is meant to be done. Someone who can mix both dark and light in touch. This is a vision that I must close my eyes to see. I say to her 'draw near & unbundle me.'

This message is both old and new. I know this to be... true."

Silence whistles through the hall. A cold wind whistles in their ears.

"Stephen," Yemaya says, her arms unfolded, her hands upon his arms, "the miracle is near."

She reaches for the door, but it's locked from the outside. Moloch on the outside.

She puts her keys in the locks. Nary a one works.

"What now?"

Arrow looks up.

"Help...me...smash the door. Smash the fucking door."

Sparks leap along the wires around his jaw. His teeth glow, there's the sound of a cosmic engine starting.

"Smash – the – fucking – door!"

Beside the beach the flowers waltz
And fate has brought
across most distant waters
The most unlikely pairing of
A father and a daughter.

Deep in the shadows of the beach Luna has stayed throughout the morning, afternoon, evening, and into steep-sliding night.

There they are, she and Thomas & between them is the green piano.

Thomas had always wanted children. Yet, in his dedication to the piano, he'd never found a wife, let alone a child & when he discovered all for himself that he had no interest in women beside them being friends & after dreaming that he was Peter Ilich Tchaikovsky reborn, looked in the mirror of his life & saw the pale moon-angled face of Tchaikovsky looking back & praying for him in his fingers, longing for a cape of night spangled with stars - why then, he dreamed of music & forgot he was to have a child.

When he was a little boy, running down the hallway to the never-running elevator, he knew he would someday have a child - a girl. He shouted it to his grandfather, "I will have a daughter!" The old man looked at him & shook his head, looked at him with rheumy peasant eyes.

"No, I don't think so, little one, but that's fine. There are enough children already in the world. Now let's take the goddamn steps again."

And then one day Thomas found himself believing that he'd never have a child. He tried his best to grow sensible, got himself a green piano, followed a sensible trail to the New Land. And now, after all that, all sense is discarded once more.

Now, he does know he's to have a child, one full-born already. This is she. That's what he actually says: "This is she."

He'd learned his English from a Grammar book & although his accent is heavy, his sentences are light & filled with case agreement & words match & all words agree with necessary words. O, he loves his English words. But now his favorite is such a simple word.

"Daughter," he says.

Luna stares at him.

"Only a few questions if you want to take over the parental thing." A pause. "Do you eat pressure fried chicken?"

"I am a vegetarian."

"Do you watch TV?"

"Only the one inside my head."

"Why do you think I'm your daughter?"

"I dreamed of you when I was a little boy & you my child would be…"

"It's enough. Were you running with an old man when you told him this?"

"Yes." His eyes fill with tears, not yet leaking down the cheeks.

Quiet – welling.

"How did you know?"

"The songs, if I play long enough, they tell me what I'm to do. Who.." He winced a little. "I'm sposed to do it with."

"Do you know about grammar?"

"Don't need it. What I need is a raft & you & your piano are needed on the raft. And I won't call you *father* – it's not a word I like. But, I know I am your daughter. Thomas, we've work to do."

And, of a sudden, the world has changed. No more to be said, no tendrils of common sense remain. He nods & goes to help his daughter. On the viridian top of the piano there are fresh red roses & the scratches of the widow's long lacquered nails. Thomas has dragged over a patio heater & the blue propane is a beacon in the night. The piano stays dry while Luna nods, for this is the time, she says. And coiled around them, the polypropylene ropes, the hemp ropes; and the staple guns and the nails and the hammers & a bunch of lawn chairs.

He and Luna work side by side upon the seat, their hands lifting over the keys, with the light of the propane heater hissing shadows across the white keys and their hands lifting & they look into each other's eyes and Thomas feels as if he may faint. For he sees, instead of pupils, that in the left eye is an upper garden and in the right eye is a lower garden & there are steps; he swears he sees steps. Above the steps, a single star forms over a small house where the central beam was once used to hang a woman known as a witch.

And he thinks *witch* and he shivers, like he used to with the Hansel & Gretel story, until he realizes that Luna is herself a witch; a witch with hands above the keyboard. And is this a witch with the smile upon her face? Is this a witch, where the music is so deep within her that it overflows into her hands & is this a witch who nods and smiles & is this witch his daughter?

"Yes", she says," ...this is. That's me. Just a piano-playing witch. And now that I've heard the splintering of locked doors it is time for us to play."

"Play? What?"

"Music that will bring the necessary folk to us & wood to us & provide us with delights for the immense journey."

Thomas always complains that English doesn't growl enough when you need it to growl; no sharp little spikes of high anger, no rolling rip-up of tundra in one word. But behind the words? Thomas now sees faces, gurneys, wood, spirits, towering sliced flames the color of old cheddar, & those flames burn throughout the world. Before his head can figure out what to say, his hands remember.

And he is playing piano with a witch & the music is sweet & it curls around them & spirals & tips & gyros throughout Seattle & along city streets & in the front door of the Halls Of Memory otherwise known as a hospital & takes the elevator & arrives just as the door greets morning as it starts splintering & spitting flakes outwards...O...jagged shards of wood.

There's snow on the floor of the hospital corridor.

No big deal: not the pretty Vermont snow of 1925 still drifting through the Internet. But the been-there-a-thousand-years snow. Some cigarette butts, two long smokes thrown down, with wet stripes running up the side to the filter and ash too tired to go black, and there's a couple of roaches ground down till their heads popped. A dog has pissed against a rusty red fire hydrant that looks as if it's been there forever. And then the hall changes half-way down. Just before the fire exit there's an old-style wood sled, around seventeen feet long, and stacked with longers of wood. The sled has stopped where the edge of the drift melts down the stairs. The wood is so old it's grey.

Seeing the sled there in the hospital corridor is weird enough – but what's truly strange is the look of the Newfoundland pony hooked, and jingle-belled into the stays of the wood filled sleigh behind him. The pony has a slightly crazed look already, but the smashing of fists against the closed wooden door doesn't make him freak – he's that kind of critter. Fortunately, whatever force brought this pony into the hallways was considerate enough to leave green- to- yellow Newfie hay across the top of the stairs.

So, Blackie, the errant horse can now chomp away, drop a momentous shit in the hospital hall & watch the door while steam hisses from the snow. Besides, he's interested in seeing what's happening to the door. He's always had a healthy equine curiosity & there's a lot to see there.

First off, the fist-pounding heats up the door, making paint bubble & blister & stipple in the way that clapboard reacts when a house fire gets ready to burst through. For a while, the paint clings to the wood like an old blister clings to a yellowed heel on a sharp shaled beach. Then it peels, folds over itself, and rolls down like an upside-down *film-noir* blind on the office door of the late Phillip Marlowe. Snap. Roll. And beneath this –?- well, an array of different types of wood, shows what we miss if we open and close a door a few thousand times without really looking. We never get a good glimmer at the door.

That's what Ern says and who am I to argue with Ern Shepherd? No one that's who.

Hang on, this deep in to our yarn, and still we're just getting started. Somehow, Phonse Skiffington (a sometimes psychic short-order cook in Newfoundland) is dreaming next to the former ghost of Susie Hopkins , and not only is this happening right now and in the recent past in Seattle , but it's, at the same time, happening right in George's Cove In Newfoundland – and as Phonse dreams he sees a door, that's every bit as real as his farts & in the past & in the future & all this is this happening at the same time, like a tablecloth laid on one table in his snoozing brain.

The Seattle door itself was made by a retired stevedore from Ladysmith who – for his hobby – spent all his life, liberating wood from the ballast of foreign ships. He knows, of course, to replace the wood with equal weight so the frigging frigate wouldn't do a flip mid-ocean flip – he was not a company so he cared, he was not a corporation so he loved life and was careful to replace what he took. That kind of guy. And he loved wood.

In the door is pressed together some deep piano-quality Mahogany & there's bleached Hawaiian driftwood shouting *Mahalo* as it splits, and the sharp sap smell of Cedro Macho joins it. The sections of Coyote Wood look like they're smeared with honey; the grain's still warm. There's Purpleheart with waves of violet Dna-Rna-entwined patterns. Hot on the fingers. And ready to sail home is *Guapinol*. All round the edge, wood splinters outwards, leaving the door itself, like it accidently got caught in the Friendly Giant's Salad-Shooter as it was spraying fragments into the hall; blowing wood chips over the load already on the sled, dusting the phlegmatic horse.

O…sweet Blackie the Newfoundland pony. One minute in 1957 he was trudging along the road from George's Cove to Outer Harbour. There was Amador & young Phonse, and younger Obadiah, and they were all happily smoking, as only 11 year olds can smoke in the 50s, great flaming clumps of Target Tobacco jammed into Vogue papers, when the sled & Blackie & the load of wood all got caught in a time-wind.

"Lord Jumpin' Dyin' Reevins," said Phonse as his father's sled vanished into time altering gusts. "What in the name of Jesus will father say?"

The 1957 time-winds were very strong that year, and blink, they took sled & spruce & fir wood as fast as a bubble of sap bursts in a fire, or when eleven year old teeth bite a tree. Pop. Blackie's gone.

Phonse wakes up with a " My God, Susie, what a dream I had."

But his dream continues, in Seattle. Recent-now Seattle. You know what I mean – All at once, naturally. All at the same time.

Of course.

Eve's hands blur like *The Flash* assembling a clock, and the strobing of Eve's delicate fingers smokes along the panels, and the door shivers but doesn't start fully coming apart until a metal chair, slammed by Gabriel, hits & the fire-ax that Yemaya uses does slam thru the heat & thru the wood. Queen Mab and Arrow have a bench and they run it at the door to smash their way even further through.

Next, Stephen runs & like a Kung Fu movie he, feet first, crashes right out the door.

Once through, they all pitch into a hallway snowdrift, with their hands bleeding & one by one, are stilled and gape-mouthed into silence as they feel the granulated snow, the dust, and see this strange & small & champing pony.

Just then Dr. Summers, the good doctor, skids around the corner, followed by his shadow Moloch (who is for the first time seen by all.)

"What the fuck?" is the good doctor's necessary question.

Arrow knows what's going on. His hands curl. His head starts to fade.

"The cave. We're going home."

And the good doctor skids around the corner.

"Where the hell are you going?"

"Who the hell is with you?" is Stephen's equally necessary question.

The doc looks behind him, and sees – well, a different version of himself. The other version has no mouth, only the light and shadow reversed.

"My ex would like him," says the doctor calmly. "He has no mouth. Allow me to introduce my shadow friend, Moloch."

Now he remembers what the soothsayer had to say, what the chart foretold & exactly how much of a schmuck he was not to have asked any questions.

Moloch, himself, bows - startled to be seen. His invisibility vanished like a fallen Harry Potter cloak, he's not used to social activities. Having no mouth he's also unable to speak.

He writes in the snow, with a shadowed finger: "Glad to meet you" adds a smiley face & as he writes, he feels the warrior leave. His arms relax, his eyes glow blue coal on fire, but only Yemaya embraces him. She is the first ever to touch the shadow, and he'd sing for her if he had lips, a voice. Instead, he cries a little.

Arrow, looks up at the ceiling. It's as tho' he can now read graffiti in the sky.

"We're off to build a raft. Let's follow the music."

"With what?" asks Queen Mab?

"Seems to me, your highness, that we've a horse and a load of wood. We've shattered the door, and no matter how weird this place has become, I'm pretty sure someone who'd like to lock us up will soon be along."

Stephen Lo, is dancing around doing random kicks. First time he's smashed his way thru a door and, O, but it feels good.

Blackie takes another dump and the snow once again steams.

Arrow, as if a thousand years and a million cave quests have led him here, goes to Blackie. He clicks his tongue against the roof of his mouth & takes the bridle, and smoothes the marlin-rough mane.

Yemaya reaches out, and touches the horse's brow, as if electricity is pouring through him. Like Gabriel, Blackie also bucks & buckles, and his eyes spark.

"First we find a piano at the beach. Then we build a raft, and then we float away from Seattle. Easy."

Queen Mab spins and spins.

"Home." That's all she says.

And all of them with armfuls of wood, streel towards the end of the hall. All say the very same thing.

"Home."

Arrow leads the horse towards the freight elevator, as everyone else stacks the door's fragments onto the load that Blackie drags. And how does Blackie feel about all this? Pretty good is the answer. The way it works for horses, in particular for Newfoundland ponies, is that they see what people think. And he can clearly see into Arrow's image of getting into the falling big room & then going out the door.

Blackie wants to get outdoors, for the hospital stinks, just like the Vet did that time he tried to cut his balls off. And failed. Newfoundland ponies can kick fast. One of Blackie's favorite memories is of hearing Phone's father saying, "Jesus, he's killed the doc." A pause. " No, just ruptured him."

Stephen remembers something his uncle, old Skipper Lo, had taught him in those last years when the old man was on his way to Los Angeles. A simple thing, really, a bit like digital editing. You imagine something else that you'd like to replace the very place where you are. Then, after making a few passes in the air, you can paste the desired world ahead of you as you go. That's an easy way to do invisibility & the old man had thought it might come in handy for other tasks.

Well, it does, for sure.

Stephen makes the passes, and then selects a section of the snow in the hall. He opens the elevator door, makes a few more passes and, then, pastes the drifts inside.

Bingo! The elevator has the snow duplicated, right down to the dead smokes and the crushed roaches.

Blackie isn't surprised. He likes this group. Dragging the wood, he goes kitty-corner in the snow-carpeted elevator, and all the other assorted oddballs clamber in.

Queen Mab, herself, makes a few passes in the air, and suddenly there's lights all along the wood.

"Good one" says Arrow, thinking that she's strung a few Christmas lights along the longers, but then he notices a whirring, much like moth's wings near the lights, and decides he'd save a second look till later.

He feels something he couldn't see in focus suddenly, with a slight bumpy landing, pitch upon his shoulder. There's a light, he hears a whir of wings and a slight whisper that sounds familiar in an unexpected kind of away, and then they're at ground level.

Stephen makes a few more passes of his own in the air, and Eve seeing what he does, duplicates the moves & the snow spreads twice as wide & down the street they step, whirring lights & all, into the Seattle sunshine.

Sunshine?

"Just a bonus" answers Stephen to Yemaya's question. And she joins in – duplicating the passes she saw them doing.

The snow spreads, Blackie, trudges, glad to still have his balls and to be in Seattle, with snow to dent under his hooves. he loves the feel of the sun upon his black mane.

At the side of the hospital, an ambulance is frozen in the middle of a turn, caught in mid-light-beat. Old folks are hanging in the air next to the door, around the corner where the greengrocer, forever juggles frozen apples. Snow falls in front of Blackie.

He drags the wood, and wishes that someone would whistle.

Like the cast of *Glee* doing a *Sound of Music* soundtrack, the merry travelers all start whistling and making simultaneous passes in the air.

Even Moloch tries to smile. The absence of a mouth hinders him a little bit. Time pulses in and out. Once in a while, the time-slip happens, and a street gang suddenly falls back to earth in full movement, whipping out guns and aiming them, until Moloch sends a black beam of light from his delighted eyes, and obliterates them all. Just a few smoking Gap-Air sneakers left near a snow-fort.

"If I only had a mouth..." despite lacking one... he tries to sing. This beats hell out of skulking around behind the good doctor, writing in his chart when he falls asleep.

He hardly can fathom what's happening, but he likes it.

Blackie lets out a massive fart, they all turn away, and the good doctor suspects that there's a lot more in his chart than he'd ever dreamed of.

The pony hears a piano playing Rachmaninoff's version of the *Chopin Nocturne Op. 9 No. 2* & turns towards it, the trail of snow leading and following the sled. Everyone follows Blackie. They know this is a critter who leads the way.

And why would he follow this sound?

Well, Phonse's father, back in 1956 Newfoundland, believed that Blackie was too small, and that he'd grow if the right music was played to him. This is before he sailed into the sky in a Ship of Ice, to vanish for many decades. In 1956 he's home from sea, and has an old wind-up gramophone with one record and that record was Rachmaninoff. In particular, his playing *Chopin's Nocturne Op. 9 No. 2.* Day & night it hissed its music on the old gramophone , yet Blackie never grew any bigger. However, he grew to love that music, and would beeline it right to the ocean whenever he heard it.

The music evoked a need to watch the sun on the waves; to see it leave again as day melted into night, and to observe ripples of stars, spreading radiantly across the water. Again & again his mind would replay it. Phonse's dad was an understanding man, and would lug along the gramophone & crank it for the pony & let Blackie sit there for hours. He enjoyed watching the pony observe the ocean while Blackie mused about the way that creatures without hooves could play the piano.

The Newfoundland pony's tail would sway in perfect baton beat to the music and, truth to tell, Phonse's dad (Skipper, or no Skipper) would sway as well. This did nothing to enhance his already dubious reputation in George's Cove. But, like Phonse, he didn't give a shit.

Back in Seattle, as soon as Blackie changed direction towards the ocean they passed an alleyway near Pike's market, where there was sleeping one homeless woman, Jockey-weight-small, yet steeplechase tall, under neatly stacked copies of the old print-edition of *The Seattle Post Intelligencer.* In her dream she hears music. She awakens & unlike everyone else around her, she's not frozen in time.

Gladys sees the troop, the sled, the horse, the doctor and the shadow doctor, watches crows drop from the trees to pitch on the load of wood. Folding her antique newspaper neatly, she looks at the daytime moon and smiles.

"I bet that pony's name is Blackie" she says & follows in their wake. A traffic policeman is frozen in time, and she checks his package with an absent-minded squeeze as she drifts by. She's very happy that a time-wind blew her backwards from the future Los Angeles all the way to the cool air of Seattle, the sweet salt smell when the wind's just the right way. The frozen moment of time where exhaust & diesel fumes curl back into themselves. She always likes it when a time-wind blows her to Seattle.

"I'm back" she says, and so she is.

What seemed it would be the hardest part – how to get the Piano to West beach - proved to be the easiest.

Somehow, as Luna and Thomas grew entranced by the weaving of their fingers on the keyboard, they lost sight of where they were. It wasn't so much that they moved the piano, as that they made time and space stay still around them. Anyone knows that the earth turns, and if something gets to hover & remain still, it's just a question of truly pausing in order to set what's stood still, delicately back down on the speeding earth when the ideal moment arrives in the here & now.

The initial nano-second lift off was a bit odd. No more leverage on the heel to assist the pressing of the pedals, as there was nothing to rest the heel upon. There was a peripheral blur as they & the piano stood still while the world flew by their flying fingers. The fact there were no intervening buildings made things smoother and prevented the inevitable splat of bones & flesh & piano, the running down of blood & tissue & piano wood & wires, over the side of a "Rent Scuba Equipment" stand – to say nothing of the obliteration of the stand itself, yellow tanks strewn all over the beach.

In a blur they arrive. First: there was the deserted beach. Second: the out-of-nowhere combo of piano *and* piano players. Third: a waterspout that counterbalanced the arriving piano did appear simultaneously & stayed to watch the show.

Slouse-o: time tipped again & the piano pitched, with the slightest of jars, enough for Thomas & Luna to look up & see sand, ocean & an approaching path of snow that unrolled right to the keys of the piano.

Thomas was a little unused to such shiftings, but Luna had early in the journey adjusted to the unusual. She continued playing. He had to pause, & watch the arriving streel of visitors stagger into view like a poor man's road show of 'The Seventh Seal.' All at once there's snow across the ground, a Pony dancing to the Nocturne, and there's a woman with moon-light trapped inside her eyes, walking bowlegged behind the main parade as it approached.

"If I've died," thinks Thomas, "then it's much better than life."

Then he's dragged back into the keyboard again, like an initially reluctant audience member who finds himself onstage, clucking chicken-style at a Stage Hypnotist's show on a vast Cruise liner.

Same feeling, so he plays that into the song.

All Blackie wants to do is listen to the music and gaze at the waves & that's what he decides to do.

The pony stops so abruptly that the wood slides forward.

Gladys arrives at the crucial moment & with an "Allow me," takes over from Arrow, unlooses the staves, puts her arm around Blackie's Mane & together the horse and the former steeplechase jockey watch the sun begin to set, as they lean towards each other and watch the sun dip in the sea.

"Well, at least he's looked after," says Yemaya.

Thomas keeps playing, and Luna goes over to start untying the wood.

"I'm guessing you're here to help me build the raft?"

No words are needed, as hand-over-hand, they begin dragging longers towards the ocean.

The Scuba-school attendant having finished, with her drifter boyfriend, a monumental moose-toke, looks out the dirty window of their shack. Takes in the new arrivals. Lucky for them, her boyfriend had read "The Adventures Of Huckleberry Finn" and had also spent endless summers refining his version of the perfect raft. His girlfriend had a father from Canada who'd been a Petty Officer on *H.M.S. Magnificent* on her round-the-world voyage. On that particular voyage, the dad had been so engrossed in tying the perfect knot that he went AWOL, ending up in San Diego. He'd hitchhiked up to Seattle & found a place to tie endless knots, spawn thirteen children between tying knots, and died last year leaving his favorite bongs to all the kids.

Long story short, the kids pitched in, and passed the smoke, and together tied all the necessary knots, as the raft was made circular, with wood laced in twelve pie shaped sections. A triangle in the center held the mast (which had a pinwheel on top.) Around the triangle, there was a square of Coyote wood. The thin spruce was buckled into a circle & finally all hands helped lift the piano to the raft.

Thomas not wanting to interrupt the reverie of Blackie & the motley crew, kept playing. The scuba sweethearts carried the bench with Thomas, while everyone else lugged the piano. Rachmaninoff would have been delighted, would even, thought Thomas, have set sail with them.

They waded in cold water, and all felt the ocean grip. 'Twas in an old way, which tugged using forces far beyond the usual. A whirlpool, as if attracted to the music spun like an old-style 78 rpm.

The whirlpool which zoomed along the shoreline had such power that it shifted & released a few time-winds of its own & one of them's the 1957 special, that goes straight ashore and sends Blackie back to the fifties version of George's Cove where the happy Pony arrives at Phonse's place just in time for supper and a serenade of, naturally, the *Chopin Nocturne.*

Another errant time wind grabs Gladys, and spins her bow-legged self like a wishbone in the sky. It carries her over miles & time to drops her near the Los Angeles version of The Mockingbird Motel. Still whistling, she picks herself & whistles a nocturne for the post-earthquake moon.

All are aboard the raft as the waterspout, bored with time-winds winding it, readjusts to the shape of a hand, scoops under the hull, & roars across the water just as Seattle wakes up again. The good folks of the stretched out town, awaken to the sight of a moon-lit raft, a baby grand & various oddballs, being open-handedly carried by a spout from West Beach to the awaiting world that lives beyond the most.

And everyone looks at the tornado-fingered hand of music as it angles and spins along the beach. It is purple, and it is green, and it holds red & black & silver has and colors that none had seen before but hope the late-nite news will explain. (Which it doesn't)

Our scuba sweethearts go back inside the shack, and we close a gentle curtain on their activities.

The Fourth Grain Of Rice

It was a long hour getting the raft to pull free of the currants, moving only when the tide was pulling back from the land; drawn by the moon, encouraged by Sedna's creatures, nudging and pushing. And what seemed a few seconds to the land, a heartbeat or two to those looking from office windows, as motion returned to Seattle, was an hour long to our friends on the raft, caught in real time.

All is still, until Queen Mab shakes her head and, from her brambled hair, lights shake across the raft. Each light spins in a circled sweep, some glow in the ocean below, others above the raft. And still the lights spray outward, until they form all points of a geodesic dome. And Moloch shakes his clipboard (a shadow of the good doctor's own clipboard) and various points of darkness join each light. They spin together, yin-yanging it in spirals, out – in – all around.

Arrow grins.

He stands upon the raft as if it's a surfboard and all feel the bow lift. With every revolution, another surgical-pin leaves his body. Crusted with skin and growing fiber, as each needle tugs away it leaves a spot of blood. More lights leaves Mab's hair. The whirr-winged illuminated blurs touch each blood dot. A hiss, a smell of burning, and small smoky winds begin to circle the circle.

The doctor throws his clipboard overboard, but before it hits the water, it becomes fused to Moloch's simultaneously-tossed clipboard, thrown in an adjoining arc. And before they hit the strange new waves, they fuse and burn like magnesium entering water. Hydrogen and oxygen smoke together, droplets of words, lines, arcs, graphs all fall into the sea.

Moloch & the good doctor touch; their hands are smoke & sun. Their fingers burn. Black and white smoke dna-splicing they go around the central mast of the raft. The sails billow, fill with smoke-wind. The pinwheel blurs into primary colours.

Queen Mab has an image of a basement flooding, books floating and sloshing, rushing through the Hippo's mouth towards the stars. She sees the water carry her out the gap, past the teeth, over the edge, to a frozen lawn, and the world tipping & as warm as soaked bread, she slips along the crust of the world into the lakes, rivers, oceans & is reformed upon a raft. She dips a hand into the water, her hand becomes water. Water burns & smokes.

Yemaya sees them as through a waterfall. Not the image of a waterfall, but a sheet of falling droplets, splashing on them all, warm as a tropical dream. Around, through, under and over & as it shapes & twists & scrubs them all – she can see images slough off every being. Skateboards slide & scalpels spin. An old robe drifts past & there's a water-wind of burned toast, dry hotcakes, fried chicken, scripts, a red chair, a grain of rice, a microscope, a fiddle and saw, an apron, all turning into water, and the ocean rises.

"The waterfall," is all she says.

"The earth falls," thinks Moloch.

"The fire falls," says Stephen.

"The air falls," says Eve

Everything drifts past them, joining the waves & the waves form a hand. Only an hour and the hand forms anew.

On shore only a second & that hand is seen to form.

The ocean herself is a swimming Sedna, and her fingers leave her hands, and form salt-bleeding fingers all round the new-born water hand.

It lifts, with the assistance of the waterspout, the raft & all ten fingers spin & are held still. The hand rises into the sky, near the top of the water spout & the hand spins them in the opposite direction to the waterspout itself.

All is still.

They reach one to the other as if in a cave. Water buckles inward, held by ribbons of earth & air & burning clouds. When all hands link they see in the center of the raft, an old man & an old woman. They're holding hands & begin to dance widdershins. Everyone else does dance the clock and as they do, the clock melts, and their hands tick, tick, tick.

Boom. Boom. Boom. Boom. Boom. Boom.

Boom.

Their hearts beat.

Heartbeats.

Boom. Boom.

Their old heart beats.

Boom.

And the raft is sucked towards the earth.

Gabriel knows he is falling.

The bed of earth pulls back her covers.

After The Raft has torn apart,
While all the hearts beat deep inside the foam,
each, like dead Vikings in a Northern Peninsula bog,
are curled as peat moss corpses;
they breath dark light & float with the logs
&
the earth turns them from sun to moon
&
back again.

While all is still
&
only one heart beat remains.

Only finger tips are seen.
The sun reflects in such a way

that there is scarlet and there is green,
there are emeralds, and rubies too;
there's a spilling of sacred pearls
which none may see but two:
- the writer and the reader -
as the slow, salt swell of combers grip
the tips of fingers to turn
the hand full round.

Down is in and up turns out
new water's found,
while feet thrash and kick
in a futile search to escape the sharp-toothed ground.

A gull wheels in and out of sight,
two cormorants slip by in search of higher land
& all is still except the ever present wind
that keens and tickles waves,
until the gull slips past again.
Both reader and writer turn,
chained inside the foam.
Fingers clutch the water:
water we soon may call our home.

Silk's tugged through my lungs
fire rushes up my spine;
I bend and curl in comber shapes
I make the moves I have to make
my eyes wide open all the time.

Eyes sting and weep and all I see
is light and salt.
I taste a broken nickel taste
as blood runs down my throat.

My heart feels light
and beats day into night.

I try to drink air:
just for a minute or two.
I cry!

Harts run – with hounds they play.
I hear them pant and, deep in forest
shadows sigh.

I know I'll learn to fly or else perhaps
I'll
learn
to
die.

Rolled in water, rolled in earth;
we're rolled towards a dying birth.

Queen Mab is the first to wake up. The dazzling white sand so bright, her cloak as black as her eyes. She's spread her hands towards the ocean & her back senses the rising water as a warm current presses against her & she feels herself lift a little, turning towards the new sky, floating like a cloud. Raining.

Looking down, she sees herself - a body as long as text upon a beach.

Long black gloves. All turning white and black, all dots –
as her sand lips pulse once. Red lips covered in sand. Sand
washed away by her rain. Lips in sand…

…Blink…

…She sees Arrow sit bolt upright as, turning, he looks
slowly past her.

"The Hag" he says, not knowing what he means until he
remembers his father talking about when he escaped the
Hag in Newfoundland: from the days when she courted him
in deep sleep. His be-belted, knock-it-back dad, who told
toddler-Arrow, that, no matter where he went, nor how
cascaded locked he hid behind Cascade Locks, he would
take only the Hag to lock them all tight again.

He still carries the mantle of the island.

- Blink –

Newfoundland in this turned-over world has the base of
the triangle at the top. North is down below, and South is as
above.

Tick – grain - dot, tick-grain-dot.

Time stands still – thoughts do not – so they can speed –
free-form, leap.

Half in, half out of water.

Face up to a blazing sun.

Salt's foaming like white toffee against his lip.

He wonders.

Wonders if it's low tide or high.

Wonders if his mouth and nose are raised enough to
breath in the sunshine while he's staring frozen at the
moving sky, the advancing water.

He feels an arm float to rise in front of his nose, and he knows the tide is coming in.

His father, before the earth had turned, had come from the old island – even before it was called Terra Nova by the few remaining people. Those were the old days of the snow & ice & hail-grain, before it began to turn back to outward-driving snow seconds later; a turning that seemed to last forever. That time – he'd been a baby born of dreams that floated him, foam on beach, glasses with salt spray ferns drying in the sun, the sun wheeling around his eyes.

And as he woke he was numb. He couldn't move – not at all. He opened his eyes – O – that was before there was no before & no after.

And although he'd forgotten most that he knew – the few remaining tatters of those childhood days & nites now lived only in his dreams.

And, when he woke up – so did a memory of what he'd feared most as a child.

When he dream-drifted through Cascade Locks he felt the old fear that he'd awakened from a nightmare and was unable to move.

Wide-awake with such a fear – a fear he hadn't had since the early days – of not being able to move when he woke up, eyes blink open – but no movement – not even the nose hairs starting to move – nothing.

Wide-awake with unblinking eyes, glazed like a Red Sea wannabee fish, regretting the trek across oceans. All brought about because of one morning that he came home early.

Arrow was sneaking in, or perhaps out – and whichever direction he was aimed in, changed when he glanced in on his way past his father. His father's face faced Arrow; and did so with a fear so deep that it stayed burned in Arrow's eyes for weeks after that.

Once Arrow learned that sleep itself is what had thrown his father to such a strange space, he took weeks before he could fall asleep with comfort and now the sliding down a cliff edged into a chasm.

The eyes of his father were wide open.

And ocean clouds of fear were rolling around the rims of his dad's eyes. His blinkers were etched into his face - the way a craze of cracks and splinterings would, of a sudden, spider-web. And like the craze of fissures and spreading lines of stress racing down it was the same as when Arrow scraped in & into the road. Here, as he's floating twixt beach & sand, he sees Mab look dawn-like at him. He floats into a cloud at the same time as he looks down at Mab, she's looking up at herself.

In the same time-tide he crashes to the road, thru the road, up again & out thru a Cascade Locks sidewalk & up the side of the house, and then into his father's eyes. He also sees himself thru his father's eyes.

Here on the beach & in the tide, he knows his eyes have been created anew – from small chipped pieces of varnish, & glazed & cracked, they looked & look & will look askew at Arrow.

Arrow looks thru the past into & out of his father's eyes. His father's feet are tied to the bed by ropes of sweat, tied with rumpled sheets that look like twisted ropes of sand.

It is the first time, the only time, that he's felt sorrow for his father; a sympathy for his marooned dad. He'd approached that pole-axed version of his father in the days of Cascade Locks that was, till now, forgotten. And when he'd touched his father's face, the father had released a small tear from each corner of his eyes.

Each tear flowed down to a separate corner of his crumpled pillows. And when the tear touched the fabric, he'd sprayed more tears with such force that it scared the shit out of Arrow – in a way that nothing else could have.

And tho' he never spoke of it to his son, nor the son to the father, Arrow would hold closer in the cluster of his memories of his dad, exactly that moment when his dad was a boy who screamed aloud – as soon as there was breath to lungs, creak his aching jaw. "The Hag"

And he'd seen the dust leave his father eyes, drift away with the first scream, now mix with his own flaring, pulsing light – he was, himself, being towed around on fresh-minted sand. And he is different, for, as he hangs in time, he grows to love the Hag.

The stillness she offers is like the first stillness; the mind before the mind. The real skateboard. Arrow would rather die on a skateboard than live in a factory like his old man. Fuck the factories – commie, capitalist. Fuck all the factories. He decides to melt into the Hag, if this is what stillness is. He wants it. He wants the particular life.

No matter what he thought before, or willed before, now, like a paragraph on a printed page, he's moored by a sea-anchor of words, bobbing – but only at one angle, tethered eventually into a circle.

He could & will feel himself sobbing against the tremble of his lung-sails. He's printed into stillness like a paragraph on a page. He couldn't move, bobbing around the circle of the sand. He can't move, simply observe – he's a grounded sled with eyes. So much is his body a part of the sand, that he can only shift as the sand itself. He's a sand person from the sand planet.

Okay. He thinks.

Here.

Now.

Okay.

And he feels that Sedna's comb is now & then & once-upon-a-time combing him from his own hair.

Here. Comb.

Now. Comb.

Then & now there's a sense of movement.

Here. Comb.

Mab feels sand – she moves like sand. Tide combs her.

Eve holds the comb. Combs her ribs like seaweed will & did & once did comb her ribs.

Thomas feels coral keys beneath his fingers and next to him is his daughter.

Luna combs the moon. The moon combs Luna.

The man with the Black & Blue Jacket & the buttons of stars is at a baseball game. He knows he's being watched. Right after he says "Move It Shadow Boy!" he looks to the side and sees a woman writing in a steno pad.

He thinks, "she's writing about me!

O...

...She writes of me!"

And then he falls through the Milky sky, and his hands write an ambidextrous writing. The Left hand writes – "The End," & his Right hand writes "The Beginning."

Both hands write *The Hag*.

So still – he writes with stardust on home base.

Arrow does not rise above the sand again. Instead, also still, he sinks through the fine grain of the dunes. His body is the sand; the sand sifts through the shaker of his body, sand drawing sand – sinking, easing.

Slow.

He floats in sand. Floats with rocks like wooden disks on a strange electric net. The earth is water.

O...

...says Yemaya – "The water is sky."

O...

...says Stephen Lo, "The fire is water warm & comforting and I can breathe water and sand as if it's air. "

All feel the Planets, the Stars, the Sky beneath them.

Beneath Ern's back he can feel a winding rope, tugging on him as if he's the wheel of Coaker's-engine. He reaches towards dead Maud.

O...

...back on earth they're turned like a flywheel on the rack of the earth, and spun back, and they hear, like the biggest one-cylinder of all, the universe coughing and almost catching with its breath-hooks the wind of sand and humus.

The red chair is by the table & I write on my rice paper. The sidewalk moves like a moving sidewalk & all have heads of light, sun-faces, moonlight-hair: combed by sea combs.

The Hag lets me be still.

Boom...

...om...

"...My heart! My heart!"

The table holds my pages. Nothing else is in this room. It fills with water; light bounces through the window; my hand tires. I hold a quill, a pen. I lose my name but not my words.

Arrow's face presses fire against igneous rocks; and in the rocks he can see his father's eyes. Rocks – no pupils. Easter Island dents. The rocks look at him and somehow, Arrow knows that the rock is what creates. He can hear their creaking words step-dance like a dancing Gargoyle poet – O

– The Hag holds Gargoyles who dream of beaches & waterfalls & rocks & volcanoes & Maud & Ern & a writer & an empty room. Everything burned out of it – everything except words.

Arrow isn't scared.

For one of the very few times in his life, he's happy.

If this is 'it' – he thinks – If I am held forever within the body of the Hag, if this is one of her multitudinous wombs, then I am glad to be in such wombs.

Forever & ever.

O…

…all of them, caught in a circle in the endless cave: caught in the circle of the suns & moons & hair slicked back as the space probe goes through all their belly buttons. As it beeps slowly back to the earth, we are all happy to die, to be vortexes spiraled, stacked like triangles inside any number of vortexes.

All of us, in all places, in all times, caught by earth; all of us able to breathe sand & flowing rock … If this is it, if I am held forever in her rocky arms, with her grainy hair above me…I shall be happy.

Boom. My heart fills an empty room.

Boom..beat…Boom

Hand still writing.

Faces below look up at this small window. My window flares.

If…

…this…

…is…

it…

The word looks at me, and I look past it to one dot.

I hear.. and when I hear my hand slows. I hear and all the uplifted faces fare...

I hear Arrow.

And 'tho Arrow cannot send even a tremor to his lips, he smiles.

And the rock knows it's melting around him, pumiced love.

Lava flows into the beach's sand & the fine dust drifts like glass-filings across Spinoza's glassine head. Arrow's head can feel itself reforming. He chill-air-feels the hairs on his arm join the Hag's downy arms, & Sedna's kelp is their arm-hair & it wraps together & tears tufts of grass from the beach. He lies as still as sand-surf. His mothers rock him – for he and the earth are born by the twin mothers – he links them, his body crackles & he is happy to drown in the waters of the world, to breathe in & out the waters of the world.

Snug as a blood-pressure cuff.

And the water rushes across his open eyes & over to splash against the Music Girl: our sweet Luna.

Luna is a circle cast upon the dunes.

As still as a circle...

...O...

...Glass beads roll through the funnel of a shell against her ear. Her eyes open, her lungs & throat & all the memories of her body move like an electric eel through a culvert towards the ocean. Somehow, caught in a gull's counter-clockwise motion, the sand at first stays still, and then – the more it remains still, the more she seems to move.

Isadora Duncaned – it flows like a scarf around her neck, tighter and tighter.

Their eyes – O - all of them, all of a once-upon-a-time, are, were & will be nested in the whispers of Ern & the whispers of Maud. On the beach, in Seattle, in Los Angeles, in India, or China, on forgotten atolls, in burgers, spelling-spilled; under subway tracks & here upon the beach, in water's edge, suspended somehow at what thru the side-ways glance both Luna & Eve sees & saw Thomas floating, just above the tip of a baton that almost, upside-down, touched & touches & will touch the earth.

All eyes are open.

Luna's pupils are struck by grains of sand that do not hurt, as her eyes themselves go to stone. It is now the wind & nothing hurts. Luna has stopped the beat-beat-beat & she knows what is the mantle of all music…

…Boom. Boom…

…and because she's as still as sand, she can see the turning of the world. Cities fly by, continents drift again and, in the drift, in the wild music of the story-wind, she knows…

…the song.

…If I awaken, she sings…

If I awaken… if I can gather the notes from the way Portuguese fishermen gather silvern & sleek fish & do attach glass buoys to their nets.

If…

…I can net that song, I'll live again, anew - O - the earth begins to slow, and as it does, the glass buoys bob closer, cities started necessary detours.

Luna sees Vermont float thru Seattle, Seattle float thru Vancouver, past the Orange Gorillas that are the mountains of the port & remembers in this ocean, on the beach, thru this *particular* air that Seattle is floating by, with the beach, the purse, the gathering of the wood; the piano at the pier. She dreams of glass islands, mountains of glass.

The wood from the raft is burning in our fire.

We look thru the smoke, and O – we see into each other's eyes.

Ern and Maud whisper.

...O...

...we are ready...

...boom...boom.

...om

Gabriel is again tumbling, robe against his legs, upside-down in sand. No mirrors, no head; ankles caught by sand; water pouring into his nostrils.

If he falls deeply enough he'll emerge near the stars. Opening his lips & prying apart his jaw, he mouth-breathes rock & pebble & sand.

Sectioned, he becomes one.

On his wrist he feels the thin fingers of the doctor.

Boom-grit-Boom-grit. Tick-tock.

72 to the minute.

48 to the minute.

8 to the minute.

Boom-Beat-Boom.

Thomas Awakens.

His eyes feel alone – and all he sees, before the sun washes light across the sky, is a small girl and a boy with small budding horns & the girl is bringing an apple to the ocean & chomping as she walks.

The beach is newly made of Piano-Key reefs and as he sees the small boy and girl run it's as if they're played by Tchaikovsky. He cannot move, but does not mind. Not one bit.

He can feel his fingers against the sand but cannot play. As the children run, he feels the notes they make and each pushes against his fingers.

O...

...His lips touch water.

O.

Where the river runs into the sea he can feel arpeggios run thru his hands; boom-boom-beat against his sandy eardrums. Music presses his feet, his hands, his ears & runs thru his heart; blood blossoms open & when his heart explodes, the music of the blossoms bloom against the morning. In Russian he hears the Hag sing.

He squints and sees a pale woman dressed in black.

She walks along the water, approaching him.

Her hand reaches towards his hands. She holds them in her sandy hands – palm to fingers, fingers to palm.

And he feels shadows and warmth mix & then he feels in the space where his heart used to be, something new, a different beat – slower somehow – night-moon-rhythms as the full moon wheels over the horizon.

Even when his lids begin to melt and close, he sees the moon.

She is dark. And he allows darkness to touch his face, kiss his eyes, lift him into blackness & as he rises and falls, Moloch is near.

Moloch also is home. All of us, no good no bad, no up no down no inside no out.

Seriously. What a laugh.

And he plays, O, he plays in my heart.

Boom.

Boom...

One last...

Boom...

One more...

...Boom.

When Yemaya dreamed – it was as a school Nurse, flying to her death, falling from the clouds into a grave in Newfoundland. She was dropped by the turning hand of her husband's hand, lowering her into a muddy grave. He planted her in a narrow trench, cut by the same shovel, the falling edge. Her last memory dropping into mud, feeling mud on her face. Into Terra Nova, out to Seattle, first a baby, then a woman, falling to a raft, floating through a waterfall. Again.

So, when she woke, her eyes blinked open to cliffs that ran down to the beach; a beach as blond as a Beach Boy's lemon-tree hair wash. She did not panic, not a bit! It was more like old home week as she saw right to the edges of her eyes. Saw like a saw saws ice & stows it for the summer & knows how to do this in the saw-dust winter.

Two lives join together – Her death in Newfoundland, & her once upon a time becoming an angel. No big deal, no Religious connections – just an old angel, new-formed, wings and all.

She could remember knowing she was the self-named Yemaya. Her beliefs dropped as naturally as the waterfall, a quick dip into the pool, the sling-shot flight into a storm & all the while, her life seemed the same even when it changed. All her memories returned: her saving children from her school, the gathering places as we all choose now to leave, and the details of all lives joined together – braiding, shifting, ropes of snow & sand & time - all love-knotted.

She had the same feeling as she did when she turned into an angel the first time, a human the first, one life when she was only a cloud & then was drawn into earth to stand & creak & walk like a poet gargoyle. When she angled & angeled back again, there was the ache under her feet: the way her ankles felt like chicken ankles, itchy feathers, tho' none could see them & there was an ache in her wing-pods, as the winds were, folded, unfurled..

"Well" thought Yemaya, "this all makes a kind of sense."

Thru the Hospital. Following Arrow & following Blackie the Pony...there she was & is & will be memory-snapped into three lives – triple lives snapped into one – like a Swiss army knife. Not a whit of Religion – unless *this* ...O... the sacred & secular... *this* could be called religion.

She'd have laughed aloud if her mouth hadn't been filled with sand & water & air; all at the edge of her breathing. It feels timeless and yet, she swears the sun moves; timeless and yet – the ocean moves & sun & moon change places again & again until the moon spills in glorious full light across the beach, until the Creamsicle-coloured sky drips into morning & still she is still & still her wing-pods ache; that sweet ache must be released, pod-ache so familiar to the new angel. And yet.

There she rests.

She doesn't mind mixing once again with the clearing water spilling over the edges of the reemerging rock. She sees waves & fish & buffalo bones all rushing over the edge. There were old houses, cities, buckled on the underwater crust, as if found on the Discovery Channel's special of underwater archeology.

The submerged Cabot tower leans like the tower of Pizza, & is underwater-embossed with centuries of dried kelp and barnacle-built palaces.

It re-emerges all round the central mountain, as if drawn up to the top. And in her vision she sees the outline of St. John's – until it collapses, spilling back. She feels the beach rising, higher and higher – each creak of the emerging earth as Terra Nova is reborn – somehow different.

She does not mind mixing with the clear rock of Newfoundland; flesh melting, bones cracking and bursting,

& slowly wearing away eons of wear – each timeless second of wear. She dropped her hourglass when she lost that life.

Each death takes something with it – & that's the ultimate gift. Give it enough and it becomes what Yemaya looks forward to – that time when *Nothing* is the gift itself. Somewhere in her gem-thoughts is this one – hold on to Nothing.

So she does.

The moon will pull time & ribs apart in the last death. Ribs and small animal skulls; linking tail joints, coccyx-scoops, all scattering as the endless earth rolls into another form. Dust is left first on fingers, then on bone and finally on dust itself.

Flesh melts, bone stretches into filaments, netting the earth, the sky, the water, cities, bookstores, books, galleys, Vox pressed sets in thrift stores, thrift stores tumble 78 rpm copies of George Formby records….

…All grinding, grinding, grinding.

Each links with her eyes – her sight catching a cornucopia of lines & all the material floats at such a distance, and yet, flows towards her still-open eyes; the grinding of all objects into light. Light is everywhere – inside and outside, sounds, sights, smells, all permeate her body – even her shadow is burned with x-rays to become part of a collapsing cave wall.

And then she can see so far back in her life, and so little ahead.

Frozen in the sand, as an odd tableau, is Seattle caught in her tears, her parents, cousins, strangers from trams. All to be seen.

Some waitress is pouring a coffee, caught forever in that second, and then caught forever in the next second as she pours coffee over the rim of the cup and down the side, and she and Eve are caught springing up – caught in a slo-motion stop-action infinite series.

Each click-click moment revolves around the coffee cup, the floor, the shoulder pad – and around each is a spinning counter-clockwise swirl & she sees Queen Mab & she does blink & then, just before the blink – all is light. And it shifts, and sways in rainbowed fabric.

- Oh my, if she is Queen Mab – I must eat of her food, drink of her drink – breathe of her breath. But now I am Yemaya and the sun has drawn her shadows to the skin, and I am as gleaming as coal is under a midnight light.

My lips are blistered, the sun – the moon swings up and down and around like a lariat. I see a body shape imprinted in the sand. Light-black-Black-light-Night-Day-Day-Night.

Only after, during, in all of this does she think – I'll be free this time. I'll finally be through; no more traveling. She reaches out towards what appears to be a raft arriving, spilling, all aboard, being flung in different directions, but falling, spiral in slo-mo as the pieces of wood fly upward far, and then falling down as barrels, houses, fences, into structures unknown to Yemaya.

As the people of this new world fall from great heights to the old world, the wood is tossed upward in a spume of water, and each person has a piece of wood to hold and all fall to earth, to water, through air, past fires growing from the wood that's meant to burn. Four beacons form.

Each person has a piece of wood – except for Stephen Lo.

As the pieces of wood fly apart – his clothes melting – Stephen crashes into the water.

Tilting, turning slowly & fast just at the last second – cutting into the water. He turns, holding the Balsa Rudder as he wash-cycles around & over & over. His knees tucking into chest, his ankles tucking into knees, knees tucking into feet, feet turning. The circles widen.

Stephen sees the Hag when she's beneath the water. And knows that's how he may slow his dive; do the impossible He senses her presence: a shiver in the water. Black water on grey water variations in light; black water wrapped around each arm (her startled naked arm) & his knees became water & she turned, half-moon/half-sun her face,

Stephen kept diving, passing through the Hag. Her left eye poured moonlight, her right eye poured sunlight.

He has now entered the skin halfway between the ocean of the air and the ocean of the waters. She presses against him & he presses as into warm water & she enters him as he enters her. Sea weed enters the warm water & wraps them both, O...slippery, shiny.

A funnel spins them again, & they fly into the sky, maelstroming – then, of a sudden, clear as day – words spinning from their lips as they become the first snowflakes of a new world & they drift in word-crystals through my mind & your mind & into this beach, landing as snow & turning into sand: white sand, tumbled sand.

She turns & is turned towards him & melts her face to become every face he's ever dreamed of, and there's her final face, the dreamed-of & forgotten face the...

...O...!

...he thinks – if this is death. Yes! I want you – now!

The children play together.

Ern & Maud, Maud & Ern – her feet leaving crow marks on the sand, walking with a shift leftward every second step.

Ern's hooves cutting across the beach. He likes the way his feet are when he tips & to his lips he sets the pipes. Looks like a Pan Flute ; sounds like a tin whistle mixed in when he tilts his head at a certain angle.

Maud touches him on the arm as he dances. They swing around together as if they had all the time in the world & with everyone frozen in time around them, it might very well be.

"She's here," thinks Maud, not knowing what she meant by *here* and by *now* or who 'she' *is*. And then – click – she gets a few memories. The very next moment, and the Hag leaps up in her sprayed-on, poured-off clothes. As she approaches, she's Buster Keaton outside his spinning house. A water spout dances away & another & another.

Ern is impressed. He begins his own spinning song of shadows & light, and he dances his hooves so fast & intensely that until the blur eases, no one knows he's danced a Celtic Knot into the sand.

The Hag lands upon the beach as a wave splashes through her, washing Stephen out of her system as he spins startled & awake towards the clouds, like a Taoist spin-top. They split in two & he flies out to the clouds & she splashes in through the ocean to the beach.

The Hag shivers & reforms and Maud & Ern clap their hands, and eat apples. The first skin is of leaf and scales, of kelp and feathers & that becomes her cloak. The next skin is a grid that resemble nets, but each square isn't actually a square. There are circles holding triangles and pentangles, &

rectangles holding stretched ovals & they catch different colors; blues and greens mainly.

Veils of water, now wrap seven-fold to her moving form.

Her net hovers over the beach & begins to float down like a lace doily dropped from a great height; a doily that holds form. It floats while staying even, even though dipping & swaying, until it lands on a table next to the Hag. She grins and laughs as she holds up a small Japanese pot, and pours a green tea that flows over all who are crushed by earth, placed in mud, part of sand, all caught by …

…The Hag! – says Ern, remembering long ago when he was human, and had dreams that stopped all movement.

"Herself," says she – "Herself on the very day you called for me. Here am I & not delayed over-much by time, schedules, space or form.

Much to do. Much to do."

And she waves – a sorcerer's sweep, much like Zorro in reverse. One by one she gathers, as if they are nets, the patterns of a dipping stairwell rising outwards, black and laced, woven with the filigree of dead leaves, of mushroom grain, long and plume like – & day moves to night & all the web is woven.

She looks towards the sky and the moonlight is vacuumed in as she breaths in, and then she opens her left eyelid, and the moonlight spills over all the webbed forms.

The beach becomes a grass carpet of grass now & then springs & lifts all those who fell into water & into earth. Every tree of the raft falls to the beach & the shadows move & uncoil & then coil again, and there is a forest made of all the trees that formed the raft.

The trees begin to grow & carry in their branches those who have awakened from their sleep. They cannot move and yet all see everything happening – slow – so slow that each second takes a minute, and each minute an hour – but they've stopped aging.

She reaches towards the moon, and her hand kelps upwards through the ocean of air, past the flying dark manta rays of shadows, and towards the sun. It shawls maple syrup on snow, creates shadows that draw the sun. And it is day – and all are, were & will be gathered on the beach & in the water & through all the clouds & mist of the new sweet earth, awakening – and it is morning of the First Day.

The last spiral of the sun is caught by her left index finger & she draws daylight over all gathered as they flare and fade from view.

The Hag lies down and closes her eyes

In Cascade Locks the web trembles & Arrow's father is caught by the Hag. Jaw asunder, he dreams how all of them have been drawn by the ocean – the power of the dreaming creatures of the ocean – their scales, the way they do dream of land. Dreaming of creatures they believe to be of the land – those dreams send no nets, thrust no harpoons, do not poke with sharp sticks. Those innocent creatures, we who are the bottom feeders at the bottom of the ocean of air. In water, whales lead the dream song and all fish join in.

We awaken on the island.

There is a woman and she finds herself naked on the beach, surrounded by paper.

In the distance is a small motel. The neon sign is lit – beating, beating, beating.

The Fifth Grain of Rice

She draws near.
  Eve begins to describe the look of what is not yet near... the feel...

...tho' she does not give measurements.

She calls for the good doctor and he lets Moloch be the small god of angles and Moloch draws them from the fissures...

...and the good doctor now sees that in addition to the straight plumb-time & 45-degreed angles, there's now the shifting bias – the drift of steam, the way water works – prying & melting its way between the angles.

What is between all the moves is the deep center.

Arrow and the group all join in.

And angles gather – the way that a man who flies three kites at once in Vancouver makes them dip and swoop and rise like two-dimensional animated stories in a series that might be called the flying Rockettes transmogrifying into kites.

See the way these kite strings are drawn towards the center of the palm – the way the strings in the air soar and thrum, the way people's throats hum and they gasp; the way the eye lines intersect the kite lines and the way they sing sing sing.

Fly fly fly.

Yes. Angles & circles & spirals are of elemental potentials.

They form angles in stillness.

All gather & gemstones are gathered. Emptiness is bounded by rough uncut geodes, the hollow sensed as hands dip & willow twigs are sucked towards the center & there is the way cows give more milk & do lean in play, & their eyes leak corn syrup & who says cows don't cry – not me, Farmer Brown.

Crystalline glue. The core is melted, scooped, spoons of nothing.

All the pieces of the raft are used. The teak, blood wood, soft Virginia pine gone gray & worm-pitted – mahogany that sank and rolled ashore. Brought like bones in the mouths of sea lions, dented and smelling of small fish.

Brought above. As below so above. Inward & outward.

Shells are gathered and placed next to precious stones. At each corner is a conch shell of inner glades.

One crystal casket is kept in the corner of one small white house.

Inside the house is a short fat man with a fiddle and a dancing old woman in see-thru form, and they are created from sunlight and refracted gem light.

There are ghost walls and rugs and ghost dishes. Bejeweled arks seal the magic in the hexagram, netting the Tao & singing them into solid death. All able to breathe; live. All are able now to live, love, lust, sing, eat, fart, sing again …

Eve is held and reflected by the petals of her script; the dust of sugar on her cheeks. She sleeps and beats no more. She fades out. She fades in & her bed cover's covered with small lights; People leave her pages of scripts. They fold her in the counterpane, do cover her with rough-tooth canvas, a Tipi canvas.

The spirits of Los Angeles carry her out of the house and into the back yard – the deep back yard. Spirits that live in the forest carry her best script...ever. The chemicals in her swimming pool are changed, boiling milk pod bubbles. Her flesh begins to melt & she is held in a golden net – the flesh is gone, the bones are capped with gold.

Her ignored stories, the comments no one listened to – her dreams, her words float on top of the water of the pool, and a vortex forms – as above so below as below so above as below so below as above so above the pillars start the water swirling, swirling, flowing. Like floating tea candles her words float away, and letters form anew, join in new patterns.

A river forms and runs through the town, along Wiltshire, and to the ocean, and stories, thoughts dreams and the words of them all rolling down the river, children snag some of the words.

A small boy called Jesus grabs the word "love," a punk called Harry grabs "tooth-pick" and dangles it from his lip – a long font stretching the words to a point.

A little girl called Lilith takes the word "memory" - and holds it against her forehead. It glows & lifts her & the other children scavenging words look towards the sky and their mouths open and the toothpick falls from the punk's mouth and all letters do scatter & he doesn't bother gathering them for he's looking with happiness that seldom fills his eyes but now does; seeing the little girl floating with memory growing larger, with the word spilling across the sky like golden clouds in a new sunset.

"Who are you?" The people on the ground shout,

"I am Lilith, born of Eve..."

One Sunday school boy hears this as it floats over his fence.

"Where's Adam?" the gold-star Boy on the Bible sheet asks?

Lilith is rising towards the stars, and stories fall off her feet. And as he looks upwards, gold stars fall from the sky & his body becomes galaxied with such stars. "I am the stars," he says and runs along a dirt road, reflecting light. The dirt feels like a robe, and his feet are warm. Dust sparkles behind him. He looks towards the stars. All roads, all paths are, once again, singing.

"Who?" Lilith asks, "Did you mean Arrow? Or Yemaya? Or...Ern & Maud... and she floats from sight, into clouds that are foaming & bubbling & cocooning.

Ganesh, in the form of a giant elephant reclining in the lap of the Goddess waves his trunk at innocents, for there are no other kind of people. Men & Women & Children are shouting & all are asking questions & Ganesh smiles & clouds gather, & there's a new rain & the new rain is of words & they sparkle & shine & fall to earth and people can take them home. A pony carries one small boy, and as he carries the word it neighs, and a little girl has the word calf and it tries to moo. And each time they squeeze the word it tells a new story of the pony called Blackie.

They walk past billboards filled with words of love & hope & joy & sadness & shit & gold & dull & bold & etc & all the words are glued with fresh fascia-holding glue & will, do & had smeared and held stardust in our minds.

But now the sky is raining fresh new words & children gather them by the armfuls & the words on billboards turn gray & begin to burn. And the words in magazines burst into flames, and everywhere the words have been arranged to say "buy" they flare and say "give".

"Oh buy me now!" Those words also burst into flame, & the fire licks along the streets and billboards burst into embers raining, soot-gluing flame. Except in Vermont where there are no billboards.

But in the stores & in houses of those who sell & the schools that teach how to buy & the factories where people march in & out for money & the cars where people get up in so-early am to drive a long way to work & in the brochures that surround children being herded up and off to school & in colleges where education is sold & bartered & along the beaches where the hucksters have set up & in the carpetbags of words & where the jingle makers carry words & notes & in the contracts filled with lawyer's words & the gavel-words being hammered by the judges of the world & in the borrowed words of the world – "You Lie" or "You cheat" or "You Bitch" or "You bastard" ...all those words are spin-dried & they burst/ burst/ burst into flames.

But the real words?

O...

...children carry them, and they make of home a home and move inside the letters, and there is a mad, swirling glowing dance.

"Wait," says one small girl, one who chose the new word for *story*.

"Let me tell of the maker of us all & let us tell of *us* & what we will, have and now make & we shall fashion her in our image, until we, our selves, shall hold them in a poem.

And the small girl snaps off a reed & she flips it in newly familiar rivers & she writes upon the cobblestones,

& she writes upon the walls & she picks up a spray paint can & she circles it like a nimbus encircles a new saint who sleeps with a bottle of words in a brown paper bag.

She pours out words.

"Once upon a time our Mother and our fathers learned that words make trees, and trees make wood and wood grows motels.

And they made & will make a motel of all our words, and where the words do build we make an isthmus, where people grew & withered, where the Brahmin-winds blow, where the waters of the Tao settle, where all religions with all people flourished & died & went wrong & stayed bad & found God & lost God & found the Goddess & lost the Goddess & where the most powerful of the Tarot cards is now blank, and where new cards form & where they find what started it all, every book, and every prayer, and every non-prayer & where all are once more as welcome as the lowest and highest microbe is welcome on this spinning planet & where children speak in the flowing babble of heart talk & where whales sing & where dogs bark of love & where cats sing of their home planet & where flowers give voice & small boys & girls know that plants cry out – and where they hear them cry out, and where those cries become songs of ecstasy.

For each morning flowers open & each evening they close & where grocers lick their pencils & then begin to write a poem & then duck from exploding windows & carry food to other writers & where we dream the world & where we talk the world & where the world shape-shifts us all. O..

we hear, once again on earth everyone's song. All hearts beating alike, and different. That place.

Why there, once upon a time, is, was & will be the tick-tick-no-tick of my story & of all our stories & time-winds will wind to the evening of the coming flowers & where the suns dips upwards & then downward & Mother Moon shines on these words...

...Why?

...so these words will link & melt & form & see the stream & where the children are smiling & now hands are raised against children & animals roam in peace & these words have floated at least once through my heart (says he who carries this for a little while) before She sets it down & I am he & she & they & it & good & bad & the words are not only the words, and O what beats beneath such a small sentence. And when it does not beat any longer, these words shall beat.

What?

Well, to all the books that lead to all the books that grow & from all the books that were stillborn: for all the books that are yet to be & despite all the unnecessary wars, born again & again, sometimes with writing, sometimes with pictures, sometimes in a Whistling language. Sometimes beneath a magnifying glass, a microscope, a lens, as Spinoza grinds the lens & there are books in the free-stores & there are books in my fingers & there are & were & will be books in your fingers & O... there are books of our eyes & there are books of our ears & there are books we make love in & the books we drop in wartime & the books we drop *on* the war-time & the books that click & the books that talk tick tick talk talk.

They are all under one small sentence that will lie heavy and light enough & sweet and sour enough & happy and sad enough to squeeze (from under the one sentence) the close of all these books & the start of all your books. All on seven grains of rice.

That sentence now forms and your eyes place it on the page & it's your hands that hold the pages & your fingers have their own books – including swirling pixel-books & if this book says anything it says be a fool, go and let your fingers write your stories & shape them & read them to your friends & make signs & ask the world to read your books & hold them like wildflowers in your hands, and if you see my van and if you hold this books, why then we may speak & while we talk you will tell me things you did not know, and if I see your book I will laugh and dance, there are no middle men there are no middle women there is only us, there is only we.

And together, we write:

The Sixth Grain of Rice

In this final moment, as I dip my pen I raise the nib. I look and one large drop begins to (egg-tempura) teardrop from the nib. I go to shake it, but there is the face of Maud and she holds out her hands and they grow like Cathar icons, and move towards me, and I may not look away.

My arm is steady, my own hand feels large, and the drop lengthens. And next to her a black shiny sun expands, and there is Eve and there is the man with the midnight jacket and she is in the pocket of that jacket, and face after face spills into the growing ink and I touch it and I smear the ink across my cheeks and I set down my pen.

Oh now it is clear, it is not all these people who nova, nor simply the island, the motel, the world – it is me & I am written by all of you. Somehow, in this life I have written so many words, so much has drifted from me that my books have stopped, now.

I look up and they are in paper & electric jackets, and there's dust on old bindings.

Stop – my hand is filled with snakes.

Stop – the snakes beat blood, and throb.

Stop – all I can hear is this one heart, now breathing.

Start – I hear Maud's heart.

Start – Eve's heart beats in mine.

Hold – the good doctor guides my hands.

They all gather on the beach & the beach is on a page & these little letters are the shells & the word-raft floats down the page,

And the mirror is in the page & you look together with me, because the final mirror in the page shows you. And all this, my friend, even if you eat the grain of rice, all of this is made by you. Hard to believe – difficult to understand in the world where we once lived; pretty simple, right now, here.

When I stare in the mirror, your eyes are in the mirror & I look into them and see myself zip small into the pupils, and I grow smaller, and blip out, and you are left before your own mirror, and your eyes stare back and there is ink on your cheeks.

Knowing that, why are you waiting? Feel Eve in one arm; Arrow in the Other, Lilith in the breathing of the heart. Your heart, your sky, your stars.

You.
Who is this, after all my words, that I see?
Why I see the perfect ending.
I see the perfect beginning.
On one tiny grain of rice:
You.

The Seventh Grain of Rice

Maud flies overhead.
Over the cave.

Through the stars, around the moon & she's zooming towards the sweet blue & white & shifting light & dark. Down to the ocean, she rockets towards George's Cove, crashes to Ariel's deck, shakes the telescope, bounces past the *Chips & Gravey*, sees Ern falling as he dies.

She hits the earth in summer. In Fall she bounces, blown by another Time Wind, to the winter when she first arrives, landing in the arriving sled, reaching from the snow-crusted blanket towards the house as Bessie appears & Ern looks out from the window.

Maud watches the light recede into a small yellow dot against grey & white & blue-black...

...O...

...she skips to a house where she's being born, goes back thru the tunnel, curls, sucks her fingers till they vanish.

Then there's only a dot/ a line/ a zero/ a one /a blast of dark & light.

Maud's on the ceiling above her mother and father.

They are naked and sweating & her father rolls back.

Maud looks from the shadowed ceiling down into her mother's eyes.

And she hears only one sentence:

"I think we made a baby."

As she falls from the boards of the ceiling & into her mother's eyes, she spins & then rushes.

"All again?

Oh, yes.

All again!"

…Blink…

…Time-winds blow them all from the cave, back to the start of the loop.

The seven-year olds fly past snakes that have their tails in their mouths.

The red chair has tipped over, light-blown hydrogen rising does light a shingled roof, the narrows, the harbor, the ocean, the CN tower, Red Rocks, Cascade Locks, Salt Spring Island.

Then…

…the chair hits the floor.

Boom.. Beat. Boom. Beat. Beat.

Boom.

…om.

Beat.

…om.

Oh yes: all rolling down and up hills together.

Oh yes.

Into the hub of the wheel.
Neck of the bellows.
All rolling ahead, back, and stopping.

Here?

Now?

O

yes.

&
Stars are born, matter creaks.
Light emerges from the sound.

…Om…

…Shanti…

…Beat. Beat.
Blink.

…Om

The Terra Nova Quartet
Acknowledgements:

My acknowledgment section ended up becoming a small book in itself!

That's no wonder, for I'm an experiential author who trusts life itself as the ultimate creator. I wish to thank those who assisted in my work, & the honor of the gift they gave by the simple expedient of paying attention to a writing life.

Writing is the opposite of gossip. It is the logging of the infinite nature of individual life; the way it pays more attention to living than it does to the killer 'should have'.

I celebrate life. Period.

An exciting time to see the completion of a quartet that began its publishing life back in 1984, and now culminates in 2018 with the final adjusting of the volumes of *The Terra Nova Quartet.*

I've now stopped revisiting and doing touch-up. The books, dear readers, are your quartet.

Publishing details of all the books are contained within each volume, but as this quartet wraps, I want to thank Bronson Smith, the wonderful Artist, who designed the look of this series, and painted an original work of Art for each Book.

He's the book designer, and an amazing artist. His website is:

http://web.mac.com/tatt2man

I want to thank my mother & father for always being the perfect readers, and for all their assistance over the years. They are missed.

Alice Sinclair, was there at the beginning – with her expected extraordinary insight about structure and scads of other important things. She is also missed.

Roy MacGregor listened to sections of C & G being read over the phone to him and still retained enough energy to make excellent suggestions after reading different versions of the manuscript.

Many thanks, as well, to Neil Rosenberg for helping me recreate Nashville, and for his advice about the music in this book. David Blackwood, who knew how parts of the world are built, was kind enough to discuss his version of shared details. I'm also grateful to John Colombo for helping discover and spread the news of *Chips & Gravey*.

Thanks to Clyde Rose for the initial *Breakwater Books* publication, and to Tony Hawke of Hounslow Press/Dundurn for giving *Maud's House* its second Home & *Chips & Gravey* its first. Thanks to Dick Buehler for being my first editor, and my most valued. Discussions with him about my first novel were respected and yet full-out funny arguments. I miss his scholarship, friendship, performing ability, poker playing and his keen mind. And to the funny and profound writer & artist, Don Austin for the generosity of his time and spirit whenever this nomadic writer showed up. And to Adrian Fowler who always inspires those around him, and welcomes ideas and friends.

Many thanks to Jeane Whetstone who supplied a wealth of Methodist hymns and their sources.

Grateful acknowledgement is made for permission to reprint an excerpt from "I Can't Help It (If I'm Still in Love with You")" by Hank Williams. 1951 Renewed 1979 Acuff-Rose Music, Inc. and Hiriam Music. Used by permission.

Many thanks to the Franklin Merrel-Wolff Fellowship – website at www.merrell-wolff.org for permission to quote from Dr. Wolff's work, "Pathways Through To Space: An Experiential Journal" © MCMLXXIII By Franklin F. Wolff. The Julian Press, Inc. 1983 edition. ISBN 0-51-54961-1

"Three Little Fishes," © Saxie Dowell

All other songs – Lyrics by William Gough, Original music, - the multi-talented Michael Hoppé & the wonderful Joe Byrne & piano-magic man, Ralph Walker.

Thanks to the many friends who assisted on this part of the crooked journey. Especially to a dedicated reader, the late Linda Aarons, who was the first to respond to Mockingbird. To tell me, from a reader's point of view, what I was doing and who gave me hope when I needed hope.

To Len Kaufmann & Doris Dowling for friendship, art & wonderful martinis.

For Chris & Evelyn at *The Santa Monica Playhouse,* for their wisdom & love of theatre & books. And for our joint voice, the joy of group creation.

For Peter Robinson who let me sing along – a braver man than most musicians. Not only did he let me sing, he put music to it.

For Tim Webber and his ever-mutating kitchen band.

For Johnny Tibo, an artist of glass, who spotted me on a film set & introduced me to a lifelong inspiration – the creations of Indigenous people & for imparting to me the knowledge of what we newcomers owe to our kind hosts.

For Martin Martin of Nain, who opened my eyes to the ways of the North.

For Johnny Blackcrow who showed me how to fly through canyons while standing on the sidewalks of Denver. I'm indebted for the urban experience of a blinking light & "Move it along, gentlemen, Move it along" moment.

Thanks to Jay Paul Apodaca who reminded me how to paint & taught me how to use oils when we were part of The Omni-artist collective.

For the homeless African-American man in the park in Denver who said "You may buy the truth but you may not sell the truth."

For all the Angels who live on the street keeping an eye out for the rest of us.

A heartfelt, very grateful "thank you" to all those who let us couch surf on many an occasion.

To Karedwyn Bird & Paul Piotrowski. For being artists in the face of it all, and for always being ready for an adventure.

Thanks to our late Buddy, Jim Lambert for buying us a bus ticket to get to Boulder when we couldn't afford it & to return to BC when we also couldn't afford it. And for smiling when we were all crammed into Clay & Lisa's house with kids, dogs, snakes, lizards & assorted guests & gave a compliment I'll always cherish: "This is the best commune I've seen."

Many thanks to Lisa Schivone for putting us up again and again, and demonstrating not only true Texas hospitality but also the Shamanic delight of life. Unending gratitude to Clay Lambert – who continues living and being an avatar of the same spirit of generosity as his dad. And who plays music that evokes harmonic response from the skies. Thanks to Kareem & his conversations.

For our buddy Sky & his son Shane – who both know how to make people welcome. We always recognize our blood brothers. Additional thanks to Sky for teaching us how to set up our magical Tipi, and for providing the use of his own when we had nowhere else to go.

Marilyn & Clarence & Dave & Penney & Ashley & Dave – who showed me that certain Cousins know exactly when true family steps up & pitches in. Grateful forever.

For Terry McLees who hosted many of our departures from Salt Spring & always offered Celtic Blessings to help us on our way. She lives in our memory.

Thank you *Boulder Bookstore* for endless coffee, and the most browsable bookstore we've ever been in.

Thanks *Red Letter Books* for your great selection. And always having deals on the books we *had* to have.

To Master Liu who showed me the inner workings of the Tao.

Thanks to Diana Hayes for her ongoing friendship & artistry.

The Mustard Seed in Victoria welcomed me & offered food without lectures. Thanks to the *Food Bank – Salt Spring Island* for kindness & the most fun coffee shop that could be imagined. Thank you *Yellow Submarine.*

Thank you Dale for that time in Boulder when you looked at total strangers & said "I feel I'm meant to give you this..." and gave us the missing hundred dollar bill that allowed us to rent near Naropa.

Teal Maedel is our dear family & friend & we are forever in her gracious debt. Gary Snyder, her late husband, was family and friend as well & left far too early. Gary, I loved your friendship & art & your ability to argue with anyone.

Thanks to Dave Pretty and the good neighbors of Battery Road who let two odd writers be part of their street & gave us time & space to follow our writing.

The Eccleston Family has our gratitude – we raise a glass to our dear departed friends, Keith & Patti & Cindy.

Thank you, Jessica Motherwell-MacFarlane & Bill Richardson – for saving our butts and not bringing the rescue up again. Thank you for inviting us to be part of your lives.

John Ryan & Irene Phelps – who did the very same thing! - are thanked for having us over again & again. And a dance of gratitude for your always memorable parties

Joe & Hope Partington – Friends and family. Some people don't go away. And what delight-filled conversations – the ultimate art form.

Dan Curtis & Jim Osborne are gifted filmmakers & writers. But even more than that – they're our creative buddies.

Café Sole – well now. Our home office whenever we live in South Boulder. Thanks for the corner table, the generous drinks of Java, and the friendships & delights of such generous folk.

For Tom, who lived in the van across that parking lot & who gave up everything so he could read in freedom. Thanks for the endless book suggestions & for being a scholar & a gentleman.

And grateful thanks for Angie Strange & her music, her gift for life, her Native intelligence & her family.

Thanks to our buddy, Fritz Arnold, Independent scholar, for his friendship & conversations. We always smile when we remember his cherry whistle as he arrived through the forest with a treasured book he'd found at the thrift store & 'just happened' to think of us.

We're also grateful for the generosity of Leslie & Karen Coultas & to Karen's Mom, Kate Murphy, and her smile in hard times. Thanks to her dad Jim Murphy, & his nickname for me of "Wild Bill" Hope to always live up to the billing :)

Thank you Rachel & Adam for the gift of an oh-so-welcome computer when I was trying to complete *Mockingbird* while writing on paper napkins. And now for the gift of Gabi.

Thanks to Sax Francisco who put us up - twice! That takes courage. Thanks to Gregg Brown who gave us the shelter we needed in Toronto.

Thanks to Farhan Kahn for his photos & description of Dhaak Wali Ziarat.

Thanks to all brilliant people who understand that children ask real questions which deserve the courtesy of truthful answers.

Thanks to my late cousin Al Seneshen who told me about Einstein in such a way that the poetry of time & space revealed to a twelve year old boy the truth of what I believed as a child.

Thanks to the Lyons family who, when we showed up from nowhere, threw us a party, opened their arms, & instantly accepted me.

And thanks to the Stone Family, for welcoming us to San Diego and their lives. We are enriched, as our family continues to expand.

Thanks to Paul McGowan for his ongoing friendship & films & who let us carve out our tipi site & always had a home for us in our rambles.

I'm grateful to my favorite historian & master of the short story, Pat O'Flaherty, for his friendship & conversation over the years. I miss him and his inspired conversations – every day.

Thanks to the Multiversity site, for the quote, spoken by Kishore Saint in the film "The shop of the open hearted" &

Thanks – through time & space to Dante, for setting down his journey, and inspiring me to become a poet. And for the perfection of Italian poetry quoted in this novel.

Thanks as well to all my students at VIU over the years. Seeing you create in such an age, gives me extra strength so I may continue to create.

Thank you, Larry Mirkin, who despite the melting of decades since we first became friends, still values our selves and our talents. Heartfelt & almost inexpressible gratitude. And the same is true for Maryke McEwen, poet of The Beach, alumni of 790 Bay.

Once again, I'm very grateful to my own teachers:

Otto Kelland – who let me hang around while he wrote. And showed me how to build replicas of sailing schooners. And that a Newfoundlander could also be a poet.

Ted Russell – who knew why the kid sitting in the back of the class was always reading. Thanks to him, like Harold Horwood & Percy Janes & Tom Cahill who showed me that Newfoundlanders could, all of us, write books.

Bennes Mardenn helped me understand the way acting relates to everything.

And thanks to my High School teacher - Lorne Wheeler who told me (when I *knew* I was going to be a doctor) that my path was the path of a writer. He turned out to be right.

Thank you to Jaime Manrique, who when he heard me read aloud at Goddard College knew what I was writing. And supported me in that dream. Thank you as well for your inspiring writing.

Nora Mitchell, a wonderful poet and teacher, I have boundless thanks for her poetry & for being my guide at Goddard.

And to Goddard College itself – where I discovered how to return to my self. Thank you Goddard. & thank you, Susannah Martin.

Thanks to the world for Her truly beatific journey thru brambles & rambles.

Thanks to all.

I don't forget.

Praise for the Quartet:

"William Gough brings it...straight from the heart. Gough is a first-rate wordsmith. His stories flow with wit and intelligence. His unique blend of esoteric poetry and hard-line narrative shines a bright light on the human condition. In short, Gough is a true literary artist.

No collection of books, private or public, is complete without his extraordinary Quartet."

Michael Kanaly – author of *"Thoughts of God," " Virus Clans" "The Voice Within"* and *"Room One"*

Praise for ...Maud's House

Maud's House...is a literary compliment paid to a people whose richest bounty, next to the sea, is the gift of language. It is also a detailed snapshot of a lost era, lovingly developed in the darkroom of the writer's memory. ...it's clear that the richness of language as it is spoken in Newfoundland is in Gough's literary blood." - *Michael Harris, The Globe and Mail*

"A good novel does something which happens only rarely in our day-to-day perceptions; It sets down what can happen in an instant of time... *Maud's House* is a wonderful book, a treat to read, and one of the best books I've read this year, period..." - *Peter Gard, The Evening Telegram*

"Gough has a colourful, excellent command of the language – he wastes not a word and keeps his characters always human and very real. This is one author who deserves a much higher profile on the Canadian literary scene." - *Val Hausch, The Edmonton Sun*

"Let us all welcome an honest voice from the east. Bill Gough delivers George's Cove with all the clarity and depth of a period photograph, thanks to a poetic gift as straight and true as the wood plane of his old Uncle William...
"Maud's House" is not just words to read, but real matter to taste and smell, to laugh and cry over, and in the end to dance." - *Roy MacGregor, author of 'Shorelines' and 'The Last Season'*

"Perhaps the most vibrant element of Maud's House is the language, which sparkles with the flavour of the outport and with Maud's own wry wit and energy." - *Gillian O'Reilly, Canadian Bookseller*

Praise for Chips & Gravey

"It's a funny and wonderful book."
E. Annie Proulx

"The arrival of a new Bill Gough novel is like being told you're heading off on a wonderful surprise vacation: no idea where you're going, the only guarantee that you're going to regret when it's over. A gift from one of our best writers, a true poet with a welcome sense of old-fashioned story-telling."
Roy MacGregor

"A magical tale of love, told with the vivid poetry of a wise, curious and passionate storyteller."
Atom Egoyan

"Like the books of Malamud and O. Henry, Chips & Gravey shimmers with a magic that sets it apart. William Gough is a novelist who writes with the poignancy of a poet."
Michael Harris

"Love story, ghost story, country-music story, and outport story, *Chips & Gravey* is a wonderful whopper."
Harry Bruce

"*Chips & Gravey* is rooted in that marginal world of hard winters and disasters on sea and land, but it ends up celebrating life almost because of the hardship that marks all of the characters. This is an important book, another of Bill's many distinct voices."
Howard Engel

Gull Pond Books:

Novels:
The Terra Nova Quartet:
> *Maud's House*
> *Chips & Gravey*
> *Midnight At The Mockingbird Motel*
> *This Is What I Must Remember*

"The Newfie Bullet" Trilogy
> *My Newfie Bullet*
> *Poet In A Pontiac*
> *Dogs Of A Strange Town*

Poetry
Ocean Of Childhood
Shinto Poem Field
Moon Tides

Thrillers:
Panama Kills!

Children's Books:
The Adventures Of Stumpman

www.ingramcontent.com/pod-product-compliance
Lightning Source LLC
Chambersburg PA
CBHW060918180626
46817CB00004B/1309